D1229974

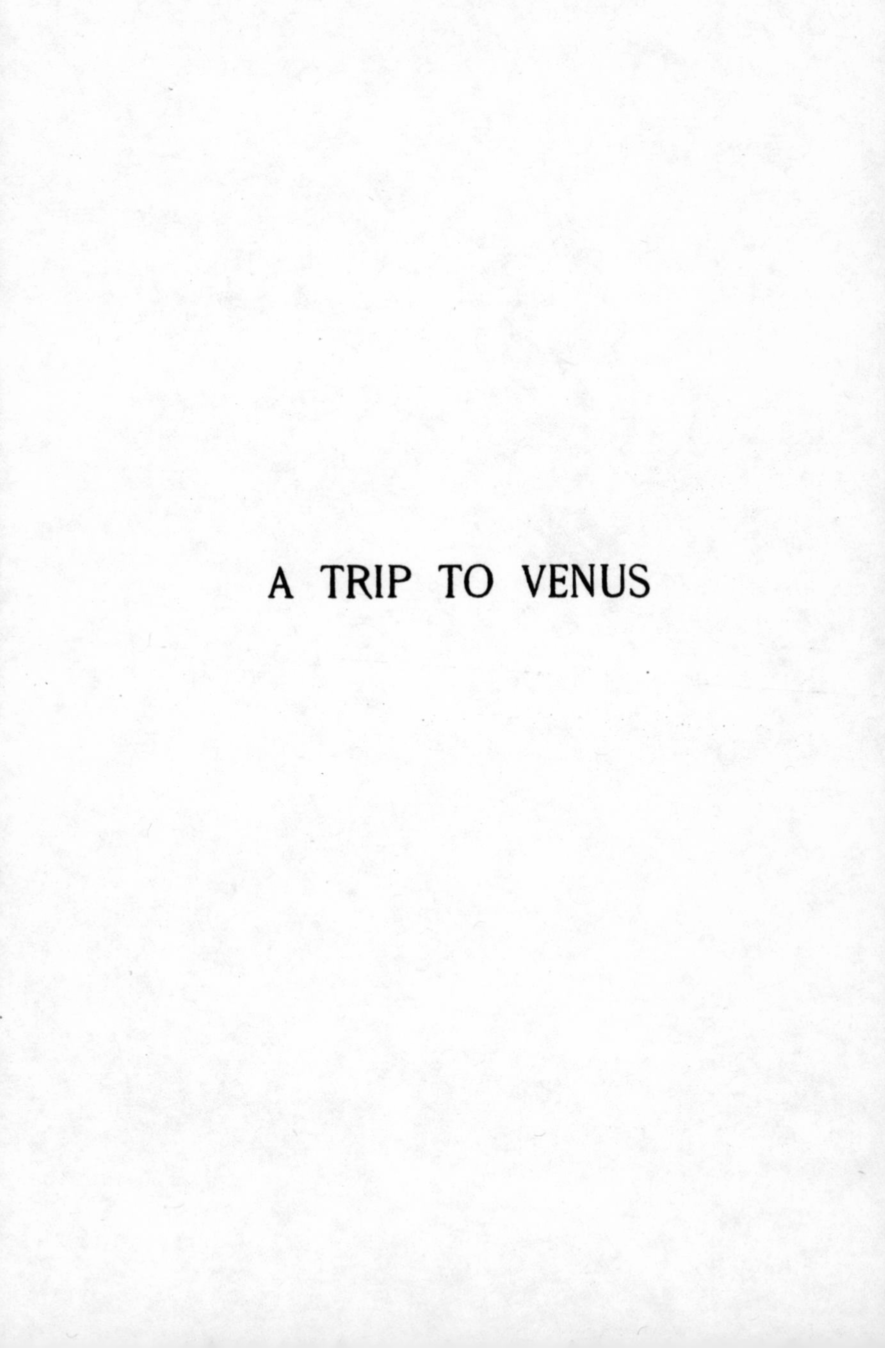

A TRIP TO VENUS

A volume in the Hyperion reprint series
CLASSICS OF SCIENCE FICTION

A TRIP TO VENUS

John Munro's astonishingly prescient novel, first published in 1897, was the earliest work of science fiction to present the theory that a multi-stage projectile would be the means by which man would be able to travel through space. It also discussed the possibility that the space craft might be propelled by rockets fired in three stages that would successively launch the vehicle and then free it from the gravitational pull of Earth. It also speculated about and discussed other potential uses of space: among them, the building of an "artificial planet" (or space station), the colonization of the solar system, emigration from old, exhausted planets to new ones, and even the utilization of space as a place of exile for incorrigible criminals and undesirables. In addition, it is a rattling good story, filled with adventure, romance, danger, conflict and bold flights of imagination. In Munro's novel, the author himself appears as a character who has written an article describing in precise detail the scientific principles of a three-stage space ship that would make inter-planetary travel possible. The article results in the author's meeting with a scientist who has built a model space vehicle and is anxious to construct a full-scale craft in which to explore the planets. The ship is built and the great adventure begins.

The germ of Munro's amazing anticipation of the future science of space first appeared in his short story, "A Message from Mars," which was published in *Cassell's Magazine* in 1895. This story later became the first chapter in *A Trip to Venus*, which was an immediate success on publication and went through four editions. John Munro was an engineer and writer of popular science books; he was also an editor and contributor to *Cassell's*, mostly on subjects scientific, from the early 1880s until 1889, the year he died.

A TRIP TO * * * * VENUS

A NOVEL

BY

JOHN MUNRO

Author of the "The Wire and the Wave,"
"The Story of Electricity," etc., etc.

HYPERION PRESS, INC.
Westport, Connecticut

Published in 1897 by Jarrold & Sons, London
Hyperion reprint edition 1976
Library of Congress Catalog Number 75-10655
ISBN 0-88355-360-0 (cloth ed.)
ISBN 0-88355-460-7 (paper ed.)
Printed in the United States of America

Library of Congress Cataloging in Publication Data

Munro, John.
A trip to Venus.

(Classics of science fiction)
Reprint of the 1897 ed. published by Jarrold, London.
I. Title.
PZ3.M9276Tr15 [PR5101.M397] 823'.8
ISBN 0-88355-360-0 *75-10655*
ISBN 0-88355-460-7 pbk.

CONTENTS.

"The heaven that rolls around cries aloud to you while it displays its eternal harmony, and yet your eyes are fixed upon the earth alone."

DANTE.

"This truth within thy mind rehearse,
That in a boundless universe
Is boundless better, boundless worse.

"Think you this mould of hopes and fears
Could find no statelier than his peers
In yonder hundred million spheres?"

TENNYSON.

A TRIP TO VENUS.

CHAPTER I.

A MESSAGE FROM MARS.

WHILE I was glancing at the *Times* newspaper in a morning train for London my eyes fell on the following item:—

A STRANGE LIGHT ON MARS.—On Monday afternoon, Dr. Krueger, who is in charge of the central bureau at Kiel, telegraphed to his correspondents:—

"*Projection lumineuse dans région australe du terminateur de Mars observée par Javelle* 28 *courant*, 16 *heures.—Perrotin.*"

In plain English, at 4 a.m., a ray of light had been observed on the disc of the planet Mars in or near the "terminator"; that is to say, the zone of twilight separating day from night. The news was doubly interesting to me, because a singular dream of "Sunrise in the Moon" had quickened my imagination as to the wonders of the universe beyond our little globe, and because of a never-to-be-forgotten experience of mine with an aged astronomer several years ago.

This extraordinary man, living the life of a recluse in his own observatory, which was situated in a lonely part of the country, had, or at any rate, believed that he had, opened up a communication with the inhabitants of Mars, by means of powerful electric lights, flashing in the manner of a signal-lantern or heliograph. I had set him down as a monomaniac; but who knows? perhaps he was not so crazy after all.

When evening came I turned to the books, and gathered a great deal about the fiery planet, including the fact that a stout man, a Daniel Lambert, could jump his own height there with the greatest ease. Very likely; but I was seeking information on the strange light, and as I could not find any I resolved to walk over and consult my old friend, Professor Gazen, the well-known astronomer, who had made his mark by a series of splendid researches with the spectroscope into the constitution of the sun and other celestial bodies.

It was a fine clear night. The sky was cloudless and of a deep dark blue, which revealed the highest heavens and the silvery lustre of the Milky Way. The great belt of Orion shone conspicuously in the east, and Sirius blazed a living gem more to the south. I looked for Mars, and soon found him further to the north, a large red star, amongst the white of the encircling constellations.

Professor Gazen was quite alone in his observatory when I arrived, and busily engaged in writing or computing at his desk.

"I hope I'm not disturbing you," said I, as we shook hands; "I know that you astronomers must work when the fine night cometh."

"Don't mention it," he replied cordially; "I'm observing one of the nebulæ just now, but it won't be in sight for a long time yet."

"What about this mysterious light on Mars. Have you seen anything of it?"

Gazen laughed.

"I have not," said he, "though I did look the other night."

"You believe that something of the kind has been seen?"

"Oh, certainly. The Nice Observatory, of which Monsieur Perrotin is director, has one of the finest telescopes in existence, and Monsieur Javelle is well-known for his careful work."

"How do you account for it?"

"The light is not outside the disc," responded Gazen, "else I should ascribe it to a small comet.

It may be due to an aurora in Mars as a writer in *Nature* has suggested, or to a range of snowy Alps, or even to a bright cloud, reflecting the sunrise. Possibly the Martians have seen the forest fires in America, and started a rival illumination."

"What strikes you as the likeliest of these notions?"

"Mountain peaks catching the sunshine."

"Might it not be the glare of a city, or a powerful search-light—in short, a signal?"

"Oh dear, no," exclaimed the astronomer, smiling incredulously. "The idea of signalling has got into people's heads through the outcry raised about it some time ago, when Mars was in 'opposition' and near the earth. I suppose you are thinking of the plan for raising and lowering the lights of London to attract the notice of the Martians?"

"No; I believe I told you of the singular experience I had some five or six years ago with an old astronomer, who thought he had established an optical telegraph to Mars?"

"Oh, yes, I remember now. Ah, that poor old chap was insane. Like the astronomer in *Rasselas*, he had brooded so long in solitude over his visionary idea that he had come to imagine it a reality."

"Might there not be some truth in his notion? Perhaps he was only a little before his time."

Gazen shook his head.

"You see," he replied, "Mars is a much older planet than ours. In winter the Arctic snows extend to within forty degrees of the equator, and the climate must be very cold. If human beings ever existed on it they must have died out long ago, or sunk to the condition of the Eskimo."

"May not the climate be softened by conditions of land and sea unknown to us? May not the science and civilisation of the Martians enable them to cope with the low temperature?"

"The atmosphere of Mars is as rare as ours at a height of six miles, and a warm-blooded creature like man would expire in it."

"Like man, yes," I answered; "but man was made for this world. We are too apt to measure things by our own experience. Why should we limit the potentiality of life by what we know of this planet?"

"In the next place," went on Gazen, ignoring my remark, "the old astronomer's plan of signalling by strong lights was quite impracticable. No artificial light is capable of reaching to Mars. Think of the immense distance and the two atmospheres to penetrate! The man was mad, as mad as a March hare! though why a March hare is mad I'm sure I don't know."

"I read the other day of an electric light in America which can be seen 150 miles through the lower atmosphere. Such a light, if properly directed, might be visible on Mars; and, for aught we know, the Martians may have discovered a still stronger beam."

"And if they have, the odds against their signalling just when we are alive to the possibility of it are simply tremendous."

"I see nothing incredible in the coincidence. Two heads often conceive the same idea about the same time, and why not two planets, if the hour be ripe? Surely there is one and the same inspiring Soul in all the universe. Besides, they may have been signalling for centuries, off and on, without our knowing it."

"Then, again," said Gazen, with a pawky twinkle in his eye, "our electric light may have woke them up."

"Perhaps they are signalling now," said I, "while we are wasting precious time. I wish you would look."

"Yes, if you like; but I don't think you'll see any 'luminous projections,' human or otherwise."

"I shall see the face of Mars, anyhow, and that will be a rare experience. It seems to me that a view of the heavenly bodies through a fine telescope, as well as a tour round the world, should form a part of a liberal education. How many run to and fro upon the earth, hunting for sights at great trouble and expense, but how few even think of that sublimer scenery of the sky which can be seen without stirring far from home! A peep at some distant orb has power to raise and purify our thoughts like a strain of sacred music, or a noble picture, or a passage from the grander poets. It always does one good."

Professor Gazen silently turned the great refracting telescope in the direction of Mars, and peered attentively through its mighty tube for several minutes.

"Is there any light?" I inquired.

"None," he replied, shaking his head. "Look for yourself."

I took his place at the eye-piece, and was almost startled to find the little coppery star, which I had seen half-an-hour before, apparently quite near, and transformed into a large globe. It resembled a gibbous moon, for a considerable part of its disc was illuminated by the sun.

A dazzling spot marked one of its poles, and the rest of its visible surface was mottled with ruddy and greenish tints which faded into white at the rim. Fascinated by the spectacle of that living world, seen at a glance, and pursuing its appointed course through the illimitable ether, I forgot my quest, and a religious awe came over me akin to that felt under the dome of a vast cathedral.

"Well, what do you make of it?"

The voice recalled me to myself, and I began to scrutinise the dim and shadowy border of the terminator for the feeblest ray of light, but all in vain.

"I can't see any 'luminous projection'; but what a magnificent object in the telescope!"

"It is indeed," rejoined the professor, "and though we have not many opportunities of seeing it, we know it better than the other planets, and almost as well as the moon. Its features have been carefully mapped like those of the moon, and christened after celebrated astronomers."

"Yourself included, I hope."

"No, sir; I have not that honour. It is true that a man I know, an enthusiastic amateur in astronomy, dubbed a lot of holes and corners in the moon after his private friends and acquaintances, myself amongst them: 'Snook's Crater,' 'Smith's Bottom,' 'Tiddler's Cove,' and so on; but I regret to say the authorities declined to sanction his nomenclature."

"I presume that bright spot on the Southern limb is one of the polar ice-caps," said I, still keeping my eye on the planet.

"Yes," replied the professor, "and they are seen to wax and wane in winter and summer. The reddish-yellow tracts are doubtless continents of an ochrey soil; and not, as some think, of a ruddy vegetation. The greenish-grey patches are probaby seas and lakes. The land and water are better mixed on Mars than on the earth—a fact which tends to equalise the climate. There is a belt of continents round the equator: 'Copernicus,' 'Galileo,' 'Dawes,' and others, having long winding lakes and inlets. These are separated by narrow seas from other islands on the north or south, such as: 'Haze Land,' 'Storm Land,' and so forth, which occupy what we should call the temperate zones, beneath the poles; but I suspect they are frigid enough. If you look closely you will see some narrow streaks crossing the continents like fractures. These are the famous 'Canals' of Schiaparelli, who discovered (and I wish I had his eyes) that many of them were 'doubled,' that is, had another canal alongside. Some of these are nearly 2,000 miles long, by fifty miles broad, and 300 miles apart."

"That beats the Suez Canal."

"I am afraid they are not artificial. The doubling is chiefly observed at the vernal equinox, our month of May, and is perhaps due to spring floods, or vegetation in valleys of the like trend, as we find in Siberia. The massing of clouds or mists will account for the peculiar whiteness at the edge of the limb, and an occasional veiling of the landscape."

While he spoke, my attention was suddenly arrested by a vivid point of light which appeared on the dark side of the terminator, and south of the equator.

"Hallo!" I exclaimed, involuntarily. "There's a light!"

"Really!" responded Gazen, in a tone of surprise, not unmingled with doubt. "Are you sure?"

"Quite. There is a distinct light on one of the continents."

"Let me see it, will you?" he rejoined, hastily; and I yielded up my place to him.

"Why, so there is," he declared, after a pause. "I suspect it has been hidden under a cloud till now."

We turned and looked at each other in silence.

"It can't be the light Javelle saw," ejaculated Gazen at length. "That was on Hellas Land."

"Should the Martians be signalling they would probably use a system of lights. I daresay they possess an electric telegraph to work it."

The professor put his eye to the glass again, and I awaited the result of his observation with eager interest.

"It's as steady as possible," said he.

"The steadiness puzzles me," I replied. "If it would only flash I should call it a signal."

"Not necessarily to us," said Gazen, with mock gravity. "You see, it might be a lighthouse flashing on the Kaiser Sea, or a night message in the autumn manœuvres of the Martians, who are, no doubt, very warlike; or even the advertisement of a new soap."

"Seriously, what do you think of it?" I asked.

"I confess it's a mystery to me," he answered, pondering deeply; and then, as if struck by a sudden thought, he added: "I wonder if it's any good trying the spectroscope on it?"

So saying, he attached to the telescope a magnificent spectroscope, which he employed in his researches on the nebulæ, and renewed his observation.

"Well, that's the most remarkable thing in all my professional experience," he exclaimed, resigning his place at the instrument to me.

"What is?" I demanded, looking into the spectroscope, where I could distinguish several faint streaks of coloured light on a darker background.

"You know that we can tell the nature of a substance that is burning by splitting up the light which comes from it in the prism of a spectroscope. Well, these bright lines of different colours are the spectrum of a luminous gas."

"Indeed! Have you any idea as to the origin of the blaze?"

"It may be electrical—for instance, an aurora. It may be a volcanic eruption, or a lake of fire such as the crater of Kilauea. Really, I can't say. Let me see if I can identify the bright lines of the spectrum."

I yielded the spectroscope to him, and scarcely had he looked into it ere he cried out—

"By all that's wonderful, the spectrum has changed. Eureka! It's thallium now. I should know that splendid green line amongst a thousand."

"Thallium!" I exclaimed, astonished in my turn.

"Yes," responded Gazen, hurriedly. "Make a note of the observation, and also of the time. You will find a book for the purpose lying on the desk."

I did as directed, and awaited further orders. The silence was so great that I could plainly hear the ticking of my watch laid on the desk before me. At the end of several minutes the professor cried—

"It has changed again : make another note."

"What is it now?"

"Sodium. The yellow bands are unmistakable."

A deep stillness reigned as before.

"There she goes again," exclaimed the professor, much excited. "Now I can see a couple of blue lines. What can that be? I believe it's indium."

Another long pause ensued.

"Now they are gone," ejaculated Gazen once more. "A red and a yellow line have taken their place. That should be lithium. Hey, presto!—and all was dark."

"What's the matter?"

"It's all over." With these words he removed the spectroscope from the telescope, and gazed anxiously at the planet. "The light is gone," he continued, after a minute. "Perhaps another cloud is passing over it. Well, we must wait. In the meantime let us consider the situation. It seems to me that we have every reason to be satisfied with our night's work. What do you think?"

There was a glow of triumph on his countenance as he came and stood before me.

"I believe it's a signal," said I, with an air of conviction.

"But how?"

"Why should it change so regularly? I've timed each spectrum, and found it to last about five minutes before another took its place."

The professor remained thoughtful and silent.

"Is it not by the light which comes from them that we have gained all our knowledge of the constitution of the heavenly bodies?" I continued. "A ray from the remotest star brings in its heart a secret message to him who can read it. Now, the Martians would naturally resort to the same medium of communication as the most obvious, simple, and practicable. By producing a powerful light they might hope to attract our attention, and by imbuing it with characteristic spectra, easily recognised and changed at intervals, they would distinguish the light from every other, and show us that it must have had an intelligent origin."

"What then?"

"We should know that the Martians had a civilisation at least as high as our own. To my mind, that would be a great discovery—the greatest since the world began."

"But of little use to either party."

"As for that, a good many of our discoveries, especially in astronomy, are not of much use. Suppose you find out the chemical composition of the nebulæ you are studying, will that lower the price of bread? No; but it will interest and enlighten us. If the Martians can tell us what Mars is made of, and we can return the compliment as regards the earth, that will be a service."

"But the correspondence must then cease, as the editors say."

"I'm not so sure of that."

"My dear fellow! How on earth are we to understand what the Martians say, and how on Mars are they to understand what we say? We have no common code."

"True; but the chemical bodies **have** certain well-defined properties, have they not?"

"Yes. Each has a peculiarity marking it from all the rest. For example, two or more may resemble each other in colour or hardness, but not in weight."

"Precisely. Now, by comparing their spectra can we not be led to distinguish a particular quality, and grasp the idea of it? In short, can the Martians not impress that idea on us by their spectro-telegraph?"

"I see what you mean," said Professor Gazen; "and, now I think of it, all the spectra we have seen belong to the group called 'metals of the alkalies and alkaline earths,' which, of course, have distinctive properties."

"At first, I should think the Martians would only try to attract our notice by striking spectra."

"Lithium is the lightest metal known to us."

"Well, we might get the idea of 'lightness' from that."

"Sodium," continued the professor, "sodium is a very soft metal, with so strong an affinity for oxygen that it burns in water. Manganese, which belongs to the 'iron group,' is hard enough to scratch glass; and, like iron, is decidedly magnetic. Copper is red ——"

"The signals for colour we might get from the spectra direct."

"Mercury or quicksilver is fluid at ordinary temperatures, and that might lead us to the idea of movement—animation—life itself."

"Having got certain fundamental ideas," I went on, "by combining these we might arrive at other distinct conceptions. We might build up an ideographic or glyphic language of signs—the signs being spectra. The numerals might be telegraphed by simple occultations of the light. Then from spectra we might pass by an easy step to equivalent signals of long and short flashes in various combinations, also made by occulting the light. With such a code, our correspondence might go on at great length, and present no difficulty; but, of course, we must be able to reply."

"If the Martians are as clever as you are pleased to imagine, we ought to learn a good deal from them."

"I hope we may, and I'm sure the world will be all the better for a little superior enlightenment on some points."

"Well, we must follow the matter up, at all events," said the professor, taking another peep through the telescope. "For the present the Martian philosophers appear to have shut up shop; and, as my nebula has now risen, I should like to do a little work on it before daybreak. Look here, if it's a fine night, can you join me to-morrow? We shall then continue our observations; but, in the meanwhile, you had better say nothing about them."

On my way home I looked for the ruddy planet as I had done in the earlier part of the night, but with very different feelings in my heart. The ice of distance and isolation separating me from it seemed to have broken down since then, and instead of a cold and alien star, I saw a friendly and familiar world—a companion to our own in the eternal solitude of the universe.

CHAPTER II.

HOW CAN WE GET TO THE OTHER PLANETS?

THE next evening promised well, and I kept my appointment, but unfortunately a slight haze gathered in the sky and prevented us from making further observations. While hoping in vain for it to clear away, Professor Gazen and I talked over the possibility of journeying to other worlds. The gist of our argument was afterwards published in a conversation, entitled "Can we reach the other planets?" which appeared in *The Day after To-morrow*. It ran as follows:

I. (*the writer*). "Do you think we shall ever be able to leave the earth and travel through space to Mars or Venus, and the other members of the Solar System?"

G. (*Checking an impulse to smile and shaking his head*), "Oh, no! Never."

I. "Yet science is working miracles, or what

would have been accounted miracles in ancient times.'

G. "No doubt, and hence people are apt to suppose that science can do everything; but after all Nature has set bounds to her achievements."

I. "Still, we don't know what we can and what we cannot do until we try."

G. "Not always; but in this case I think we know. The celestial bodies are evidently isolated in space, and the tenants of one cannot pass to another. We are confined to our own planet."

I. "A similar objection might have been urged against the plan of Columbus."

G. "That was different. Columbus only sailed through unknown seas to a distant continent. We are free to explore every nook and cranny of the earth, but how shall we cross the immense void which parts us from another world, except on the wings of the imagination?"

I. "Great discoveries and inventions are born of dreams. There are minds which can foresee what lies before us, and the march of science brings it within our reach. All or nearly all our great scientific victories have been foretold, and they have generally been achieved by more than one person when the time came. The telescope was a dream for ages, so was the telephone, steam and electric locomotion, aerial navigation. Why should we scout the dream of visiting other worlds, which is at least as old as Lucian? Ere long, and perhaps before the century is out, we shall be flying through the air to the various countries of the globe. In succeeding centuries what is to hinder us from travelling through space to different planets?"

G. "Quite impossible. Consider the tremendous distance—the lifeless vacuum—that separates us even from the moon. Two hundred and forty thousand miles of empty space."

I. "Some ten times round the world. Well, is that tremendous vacuum absolutely impassable?"

G. "To any but Jules Verne and his hero, the illustrious Barbicane, president of the Gun Club."*

I. "Jules Verne has an original mind, and his ideas, though extravagant, are not without value. Some of them have been realised, and it may be worth while to examine his notion of firing a shot from the earth to the moon. The projectile, if I remember, was an aluminium shell in the shape of a conical bullet, and contained three men, a dog or two, and several fowls, together with provisions

* *The Voyage à la Lune*, by Jules Verne.

and instruments. It was air tight, warmed and illuminated with coal gas, and the oxygen for breathing was got from chlorate of potash, while the carbonic acid produced by the lungs and gas-burners was absorbed with caustic potash to keep the air pure. This bullet-car was fired from a colossal cast-iron gun founded in the sand. It was aimed at a point in the sky, the zenith, in fact, where it would strike the moon four days later, that is, after it had crossed the intervening space. The charge of gun-cotton was calculated to give the projectile a velocity sufficient to carry it past the 'dead-point,' where the gravity of the earth upon it was just balanced by that of the moon, and enable it to fall towards the moon for the rest of the way. The sudden shock of the discharge on the car and its occupants was broken by means of spring buffers and water pressure."

G. "The last arrangement was altogether inadequate."

I. "It was certainly a defect in the scheme."

G. "Besides, the initial velocity of the bullet to carry it beyond the 'dead-point,' was, I think, 12,000 yards a second, or something like seven miles a second."

I. "His estimate was too high. An initial velocity of 9,000 yards, or five miles a second, would carry a projectile beyond the sensible attraction of the earth towards the moon, the planets, or anywhere; in short, to an infinite distance. Indeed, a slightly lower velocity would suffice in the case of the moon, owing to her attraction."

G. "But how are we to give the bullet that velocity? I believe the highest velocity obtained from a single discharge of cordite, one of our best explosives, was rather less than 4,000 feet, or only about three-quarters of a mile per second. With such a velocity, the projectile would simply rise to a great height and then fall back to the ground."

I. "Both of these drawbacks can be overcome. We are not limited to a single discharge. Dr. S. Tolver Preston, the well-known writer on molecular science, has pointed out that a very high velocity can be got by the use of a compound gun, or, in other words, a gun which fires another gun as a projectile.* Imagine a first gun of enormous dimensions loaded with a smaller gun, which in turn is loaded with the bullet. The discharge of the first gun shoots the second gun into the air, with a certain velocity. If, now, the second gun, at the instant it leaves the muzzle of the first, is fired

* *Engineering*, January 13th, 1893.

automatically, say by utilising the first discharge to press a spring which can react on a hammer or needle, the bullet will acquire a velocity due to both discharges, and equivalent to the velocity of the second gun at the time it was fired plus the velocity produced by the explosion of its own charge. In this way, by employing a series of guns, fired from each other in succession, we can graduate the starting shock, and give the bullet a final velocity sufficient to raise it against gravity, and the resistance of the atmosphere, which grows less as it advances, and send it away to the moon or some other distant orb."

G. "Your spit-fire mode of progression is well enough in theory, but it strikes me as just a little complicated and risky. I, for one, shouldn't care to emulate Elijah and shoot up to Heaven in that style."

I. "If it be all right in theory, it will be all right in practice. However, instead of explosives we might employ compressed air to get the required velocity. In the air-gun or cannon, as you probably know, a quantity of air, compressed within a chamber of the breech, is allowed suddenly to expand behind the bullet and eject it from the barrel. Now, one might manage with a simple gun of this sort, provided it had a very long barrel, and a series of air chambers at intervals from the breech to the muzzle. Each of these chambers, beginning at the breech, could be opened in turn as the bullet passed along the barrel, so that every escaping jet of gas would give it an additional impulse."

G. (*with growing interest*). "That sounds neater. You might work the chambers by electricity."

I. "We could even have an electric gun. Conceive a bobbin wound with insulated wire in lieu of thread, and having the usual hole through the axis of the frame. If a current of electricity be sent through the wire, the bobbin will become a hollow magnet or 'solenoid,' and a plug of soft iron placed at one end will be sucked into the hole. In this experiment we have the germ of a solenoid cannon. The bobbin stands for the gun-barrel, the plug for the bullet-car, and the magnetism for the ejecting force. We can arrange the wire and current so as to draw the plug or car right through the hole or barrel, and if we have a series of solenoids end to end in one straight line, we can switch the current through each in succession, and send the projectile with gathering velocity through the interior of them all. In practice the barrel would consist of a long straight tube, wide and strong enough to contain the bullet-car without flexure, and begirt with giant solenoids at intervals. Each of the solenoids would be excited by a powerful current, one after the other, so as to urge the projectile with accelerating speed along the tube, and launch it into the vast."

G. "That looks still better than the pneumatic gun."

I. "A magnetic gun would have several advantages. For instance, the currents can be sent through the solenoids in turn as quickly as we desire by means of a commutator in a convenient spot, for instance, at the butt end of the gun, so as to follow up the bullet with ease, and give it a planetary flight. By a proper adjustment of the solenoids and currents, this could be done so gradually as to prevent a starting shock to the occupants of the car. The velocity attained by the car would, of course, depend on the number and power of the solenoids. If, for example, each solenoid communicated to the car a velocity of nine yards per second, a thousand solenoids, each magnetically stronger than another in going from breech to muzzle, would be required to give a final velocity of five miles a second. In such a case, the length of the barrel would be at least 1,000 yards. Economy and safety would determine the best proportions for the gun, but we are now considering the feasibility of the project, not its cost. With regard to position and supports, the gun might be constructed along the slope of a hill or mound steep enough to give it the angle or elevation due to the aim. As the barrel would not have to resist an explosive force, it should not be difficult to make, and the inside could be lubricated to diminish the friction of the projectile in passing through it. Moreover, it is conceivable that the car need never touch the sides, for by a proper adjustment of the magnetism of the solenoids we might suspend it in mid-air like Mahomet's coffin, and make it glide along the magnetic axis of the tube."

G. "It seems a promising idea for an actual gun, or an electric despatch and parcel post, or even a railway. The bullet, I suppose, would be of iron."

I. "Probably; but aluminium is magnetic in a lower degree than iron, and its greater lightness might prove in its favour. We might also magnetise the car, say by surrounding it with a coil of wire excited from an accumulator on board. The car, of course, would be hermetically sealed, but it would have doors and windows which could be opened at pleasure. In open space it would be warmed and lighted by the sun, and in the shadow of a planet, if need were, by coal-gas and electricity. In either case, to temper the extremes of heat or cold, the interior could be lined with a non-conductor. Liquefied oxygen or air for breathing, and condensed fare would sustain the inmates; and on the whole they might enjoy a comfortable passage through the void, taking scientific observations, and talking over their experiences."

G. "It would be a novel observatory, quite free from atmospheric troubles. They might be able to make some astronomical discoveries."

I. "A novel laboratory as well, for in space beyond the attraction of the earth there would be no gravity. The travellers would not feel a sense of weight, but as the change would be gradual they would get accustomed to it, and suffer no inconvenience."

G. "They would keep their gravity in losing it."

I. "The car, meeting with practically no resistance in the ether, would tend to move in the same direction with the same velocity, and anything put overboard would neither fall nor rise, but simply float alongside. When the car came within the sensible attraction of the moon, its velocity would gradually increase as they approached each other."

G. "Always supposing the aim of the gun to

have been exact. You might hit the moon, with its large disc and comparatively short range, provided no wandering meteorite diverted the bullet from its course; but it would be impossible to hit a planet, such as Venus or Mars, a mere point of light, and thirty or forty million miles away, especially as both the earth and planet are in rapid motion. A flying rifle-shot from a lightning express at a distant swallow would have more chance of success. If you missed the mark, the projectile would wheel round the planet, and either become its satellite or return towards the earth like that of Jules Verne in his fascinating romance."

I. "Jules Verne, and other writers on this subject, appear to have assumed that all the initial effort should come from the cannon. Perhaps it did not suit his literary purpose to employ any other driving force. At all events he possessed one in the rockets of Michel Ardan, the genial Frenchman of the party, which were intended to break the fall of the projectile on the moon."

G. "If I recollect, they were actually fired to give the car a fillip when it reached the dead-point on its way back to the earth."

I. "Even in a vacuum, where an ordinary propeller could not act, the bullet may become a prime mover, and co-operate with the gun. A rocket can burn without an atmosphere, and the recoil of the rushing fumes will impel the car onwards."

G. "Do you think a rocket would have sufficient power to be of any service?"

I. "Ten or twelve large rockets, capable of exerting a united back pressure of one and a half tons during five or six minutes on a car of that weight at the earth's surface, would give it in free space a velocity of two miles a second, which, of course, would not be lost by friction."

G. "So that it would not be absolutely necessary to give the projectile an initial velocity of five miles a second."

I. "No; and, besides, we are not solely dependent on the rocket. A jet of gas, at a very high pressure, escaping from an orifice into the vacuum or ether, would give us a very high propelling force. By compressing air, oxygen, or coal-gas (useful otherwise) in iron cylinders with closed vents, which could be opened, we should have a store of energy serviceable at any time to drive the car. In this way a pressure or thrust of several tons on the square inch might be applied to the car as long as we had gas to push it forwards."

G. "Certainly, and by applying the pressure,

whether from the rocket or the gas, to the front and sides, as well as to the rear of the car, you would be able to regulate the speed, and direct the car wherever you wanted to go."

I. "Moreover, beyond the range of gravitation, we could steer and travel by pumping out the respired air, or occasionally projecting a pebble from the car through a stuffing box in the wall, or else by firing a shot from a pistol."

G. "You might even have a battery of machine guns on board, and decimate the hosts of heaven."

I. "Our bullets would fly straight enough, anyhow, and I suppose they would hit something in course of time."

G. "If they struck the earth they would be solemnly registered as falling stars."

I. "Certainly they would be burnt up in passing through the atmosphere of a planet and do no harm to its inhabitants."

G. "Well, now, granting that you could propel the car, and that although your gun was badly aimed you could steer towards a planet, how long would the journey take?"

I. "The self-movement of the car would enable us to save time, which is a matter of the first importance on such a trip. In the plan of Jules Verne, the bullet derives all its motion from the initial effort, and consequently slows down as it rises against the earth's attraction, until it begins again to quicken under the gravitation of the moon. Hence his voyage to our satellite occupied four days. As we could maintain the velocity of the car, however, we should accomplish the distance in thirteen hours at a speed of five miles a second, and more or less in proportion."

G. "About as long as the journey from London to Aberdeen by rail. What about Mars or Venus?"

I. "At the same speed we should cover the 36,000,000 miles to these planets in 2,000 hours, or 84 days, that is, about three months. With a speed of ten miles a second, which is not impossible, we could reach them in six weeks."

G. "One could scarcely go round the world in the same time. But, having got to a planet, how are you going to land on it? Are you not afraid you will be dissipated like a meteorite by the intense heat of friction with the planet's atmosphere, or else be smashed to atoms by the shock?"

I. "We might steer by the stars to a point on the planet's orbit, mathematically fixed in advance, and wait there until it comes up. The atmosphere of the approaching planet would act as a kind of buffer, and the fall of the car could be further checked by our means of recoil, and also by a large parachute. We should probably be able to descend quite slowly to the surface in this way without damage; but in case of peril, we could have small parachutes in readiness as life-buoys, and leap from the car when it was nearing the ground."

G. "I presume you are taking into account the velocity of the planet in its orbit? That of the earth is 18 miles a second, or a hundred times faster than a rifle bullet; that of Venus, which is nearer the sun, is a few miles more; and that of Mars, which is further from the sun, is rather less."

I. "For that reason the more distant planets would be preferable to land on. Uranus, for instance, has an orbital velocity of four miles a second, and his gravity is about three-fourths that of the earth. Moreover, his axis lies almost exactly on the plane of the ecliptic, so that we could choose a waiting place on his orbit where the line of his axis lay in the direction of his motion, and simply descend on one of his poles, at which the stationary atmosphere would not whirl the car, and where we might also profit by an ascending current of air. The attraction of the sun is so slight at the distance of Uranus, that a stone flung out of the car would have no perceptible motion, as it would only fall towards the sun a mere fraction of an inch per second, or some 355 feet an hour; hence, as Dr. Preston has calculated, one ounce of matter ejected from the car towards the sun every five minutes, with a velocity of 880 feet a second, would suffice to keep a car of one and a half tons at rest on the orbit of the planet. Indeed, the vitiated air, escaping from the car through a small hole by its own pressure, would probably serve the purpose. Just before the planet came up, and in the nick of time we could fire some rockets, and give the car a velocity of two or three miles a second in the direction of the planet's motion, so that he would overtake us, with a speed not over great to ensure a safe descent. Our parachutes would be out, and at the first contact with the atmosphere, the car would probably be blown away; but it would soon acquire the velocity of the planet, and gradually sink downwards to the surface."

G. "What puzzles me is how you are to get back to the earth."

I. "Whoever goes must take the risk; but if, as appears likely, both Mars and Venus are inhabited by intelligent beings, we should probably be able to construct another cannon and return the way we came."

G. (*smiling*). "Well, I confess the project does not look so impracticable as it did. After all, travelling in a vacuum seems rather pleasant. One of these days, I suppose, we astronomers will be packed in bullets and fired into the ether to observe eclipses and comets' tails."

I. "In all that has been said we have confined ourselves to ways and means already known; but science is young, and we shall probably discover new sources of energy. It may even be possible to dispense with the gun, and travel in a locomotive car. Lord Kelvin has shown that if Lessage's hypothesis of gravitation be correct, a crystal or other body may be found which is lighter along one axis than another, and thus we may be able to draw an unlimited supply of power from gravity by simply changing the position of the crystal; for example, by raising it when lighter, and letting it fall when heavier. This form of 'perpetual motion' might be equally obtainable if Dr. Preston's* theory of an ether as the cause of gravity be true. Indeed, Professor Poynting is now engaged in searching for such a crystal, which, if discovered, will upset the second law of thermo-dynamics. I merely mention this to show that science is on the

* *Philosophical Magazine*, February, 1895.

track of concealed motive powers derived from the ether, and we cannot now tell what the engines of the future will be like. For ought we know, the time is coming when there will be a regular mail service between the earth and Mars or Venus, cheap trips to Mercury, and exploring expeditions to Jupiter, Saturn, or Uranus."

CHAPTER III.

A NEW FORCE.

"SIR,

"I have read your article on the possibility of travelling to the other members of the Solar system with much interest. It is a problem at which I, myself, have been working for a great many years, and I believe that I have now discovered a means of solving it in a practical manner. If you would care to see my experiments, and will do me the honour of coming here, I shall be glad to show them in confidence any time you may appoint.—Yours truly,

"NASMYTH CARMICHAEL."

The above letter, marked "Private," was forwarded to me through the editor of *The Day After To-morrow*. The writer of it was a total stranger to me, even by report, and at first I did not know what to make of it. Was the man a charlatan, or a "crank?" There were no signs of craziness or humbug in his frank and simple sentences. Had he really found out a way of crossing the celestial spaces? In these days it is better not to be too sceptical as to what science will accomplish. It is, in fact, wise to keep the mind open and suspend he judgment. We are standing on the threshold of the Arcana, and at any hour the search-light of our intellect may penetrate the darkness, and reveal to our wondering gaze the depths of the inner mechanism of Nature.

I resolved to accept his invitation.

A few days later I presented myself at the home of my unknown correspondent. It was a lonely little cottage, in the midst of a wild flat or waste of common ground on the outskirts of London. I should say it had once been the dwelling of a woodman engaged in the neighbouring forest. A tall, thick hedge of holly surrounded the large garden, and almost concealed it from the curiosity of an occasional wanderer on the heath.

Certainly it did not look the sort of place to find a man of science, and the old misgivings assailed my mind in greater force than ever. Half regretting that I had come, and feeling in a dubious element, I opened the wicket, and knocked at the door.

It was answered by a young woman, in a plain gown of some dark stuff, with a white collar round the neck. In spite of her dress I could see that she was not an ordinary cottage girl. Pretty, without being beautiful, there was a distinction in her voice and manner which bespoke the gentlewoman. With a pleasant smile, she welcomed me as one who had been expected, and ushered me into a small sitting-room, poorly furnished, but with a taste and refinement unusual in a workman's home. A large piano stood in one of the corners, and a pile of classical music lay on a chair beside it. The mantelpiece was decorated with cut flowers, and the walls were hung with portraits and sketches in crayons and water-colour.

"My father will be down in a moment," she said, with a slight American accent. "He is delighted to have the pleasure of meeting you. It is so kind of you to come."

Before I had time to respond, Mr. Carmichael entered the parlour. He was a man of striking and venerable presence. His long white locks, his bulging brow, pregnant with brain, his bushy eyebrows and deep blue-grey eyes, his aquiline nose and flowing beard, gave an Olympian cast to his noble head. Withal, I could not help noticing that his countenance was lined with care, his black coat seamed and threadbare, his hands rough and horny, like those of a workman. If he appeared a god, it was a god in exile or disgrace; a Saturn rather than a Jove.

"Now to the matter," said he, after a few words of kindly welcome. "Evidently the question of inter-planetary travel is coming to the front. In your article you suggest that a locomotive car, that is to say, a car able to propel itself through what we, in our ignorance, call empty space, though, in reality, it is chock-full, and very 'thrang' as the Scotch say, might yet be contrived, and even worked by energy drawn from the ether direct. When I read that, sir, I sat up and rubbed my eyes."

"Your spectacles, father," said Miss Carmichael.

"Well, it's the same thing," went on the old man. "For like many another prophet, sir, you had prophesied better than you knew."

"How do you mean?" I inquired, with a puzzled air.

"If you will step with me into the garden I will show you."

I rose and followed him into a large shed, which was fitted up as a workshop and laboratory. It contained several large benches, provided with turning lathes and tools, a quantity of chemicals, and scientific apparatus.

"I am going to do a thing that I have never done in my life before," said Mr. Carmichael, in a sad and doubtful tone; "I have kept this secret so long that it seems like parting with myself to disclose it, to disclose even the existence of it. I have fed upon it as a young man feeds on love. It has been my nourishment, my manna in the wilderness of this world, my solace under a thousand trials, my inspiration from on High. I verily believe it has kept my old carcase together. Mind!" he added, with a penetrating glance of his grey eyes, which gleamed under their bushy brows like a pool of water in a cavern overhung with brambles, "promise me that whatever you see and hear will remain a secret on your part. Never breathe a word of it to a living soul. You are the only person, except my own daughter, whom I have ever taken into my confidence."

I gave him my word of honour.

"Very well," he continued, lifting a small metal box from one of the tables, and patting it with his hand. "I have been working at the subject of aerial navigation for well-nigh thirty years, and this is the result."

I looked at the metal case, but could see nothing remarkable about it.

"It seems a little thing, hardly worth a few pence, and yet how much I have paid for it!" said the inventor, with a sigh, and a far-away expression in his eyes. "Many a time it has reminded me of the mouse's nest that was turned up by the plough-share.

> "'Thy wee bit heap o' strae and stibble
> Has cost thee mony a weary nibble.'

Of course this is only a model."

"A model of a flying machine?" I inquired, in a tone of surprise.

"You may call it so," he answered; "but it is a flying machine that does not fly or soar in the strict sense of the words, for it has neither wings nor aeroplane. It is, in fact, an aerial locomotive, as you will see."

While he spoke, Mr. Carmichael opened the case of the instrument, and adjusted the mechanism inside. Immediately afterwards, to my astonishment, the box suddenly left his hands, and flew, or rather glided, swiftly through the air, and must have dashed itself against the wall of the laboratory had not its master run and caught it.

"Wonderful!" I exclaimed, forgetting the attitude of caution and reserve which I had deemed it prudent to adopt.

The inventor laughed with childish glee, enjoying his triumph, and stroking the case as though it were a kitten.

"It would be off again if I would let it. Whoa,

there!" said he, again adjusting the mechanism. "I can make it rise, or sink, or steer, to one side or the other, just as I please. If you will kindly hold it for a minute, I will make it go up to the ceiling. Don't be afraid, it won't bite you."

I took the uncanny little instrument in my hands, whilst Mr. Carmichael ascended a ladder to a kind of loft in the shed. It only weighed a few pounds, and yet I could feel it exerting a strong force to escape.

"Ready!" cried the inventor, "now let go," and sure enough, the box rose steadily upwards until it came within his grasp. "I am going to send it down to you again," he continued, and I expected to see it drop like a stone to the ground; but, strange to say, it circled gracefully through the air in a spiral curve, and landed gently at my feet.

"You see I have entire control over it," said Mr. Carmichael, rejoining me; "but all you have seen has taken place in air, and you might, therefore, suppose that I have an air propellor inside, and that air is necessary to react against it, like water against the screw of a steamboat, in order to produce the motion. I will now show you that air is not required, and that my locomotive works quite as well in a vacuum."

So saying, he put the model under a large bell-jar, from which he exhausted the air with a pump; and even then it moved about with as much alacrity and freedom as it had done in the atmosphere.

I confess that I was still haunted by a lingering suspicion of the machine and its inventor; but this experiment went far to destroy it. Even if the motive power was derived from a coiled spring, or compressed air, or electricity, in the box, how was it possible to make it act without the resistance offered by the air? Magnetism was equally out of the question, since no conceivable arrangement of magnets could have brought about the movements I had seen. Either I was hypnotised, and imposed upon, or else this man had discovered what had been unknown to science. His earnest and straightforward manner was not that of a mountebank. There had been no attempt to surround his work with mystery, and cloak his demonstration in unmeaning verbiage. It is true I had never heard of him in the world of science, but after all an outsider often makes a great discovery under the nose of the professors.

"Am I to understand," said I, "that you have found a way of navigating both the atmosphere and the ether?"

"As you see," he replied, briefly.

"What the model has done, you are able to do on a larger scale—in a practical manner?"

"Assuredly. It is only a matter of size."

"And you can maintain the motion?"

"As long as you like."

"Marvellous! And how is it done?"

"Ah!" exclaimed the inventor, "that is my secret. I am afraid I must not answer that question at present."

"Is the plan not patented?"

"No. The fact is, I have not yet investigated the subject as fully as I would like. My mind is not quite clear as to the causes of the phenomena. I have discovered a new field of research, and great discoveries are still to be made in it. Were I to patent the machine, I should have to divulge what I know. Indeed, but for the sake of my daughter, I am not sure that I should ever patent it. Even as it stands, it will revolutionise not merely our modes of travel, but our industries. It has been to me a labour of love, not of money; and I would gladly make it a gift of love to my fellowmen."

"It is the right spirit," said I; "and I have no doubt that a grateful world would reward you."

"I wouldn't like to trust it," replied Mr. Carmichael, with a smile and shrug of the shoulders. "How many inventors has it doomed to pine in poverty and neglect, or die of a broken heart? How often has it stolen, aye stolen, the priceless fruits of their genius and labour? Speaking for myself, I don't complain; I haven't had much to do with it. My withdrawal from it has been voluntary. I was born in the south of Scotland, and educated for the medical profession; but I emigrated to America, and was engaged in one of Colonel Fremont's exploring expeditions to the Rocky Mountains. After that I was appointed to the chair of Physical Science in a college of Louisville, Kentucky, where my daughter was born. One day, when I was experimenting to find out something else, I fell by accident upon the track of my discovery, and ever since I have devoted my life to the investigation. It appeared to me of the very highest importance. As time went on, I grew more and more absorbed in it. Every hour that I had to give to my official and social duties seemed thrown away. A man cannot serve two masters, and as I also found it difficult to carry on my experiments in secrecy, I resigned my post. I had become a citizen of the United States, but my wife was a Welshwoman, and had relations in England. So we came to London. When she died, I settled in this isolated spot, where I could study in peace, enjoy the fresh air, and easily get the requisite books and apparatus. Here, with my daughter, I live a very secluded life. She is my sole companion, my housekeeper, my servant, and my assistant in the laboratory. She knows as much about my machine, and can work it as well as I do myself. Indeed, I don't know what I should have done without her. She has denied herself the ordinary amusements of her age. Her devotion to me has been beautiful."

The voice of the old man trembled, and I fancied I could read in his hollow eyes the untold martyrdom of genius.

"At last," he continued, "I have brought the matter into a practical shape, and like many other inventors, for the first time I stand in need of advice. Happening to see your article in the Magazine, I resolved to invite you to come and see what I have done in hopes that you might be able to advise and perhaps help me."

"I think," said I, after a moment's reflection, "I think the next thing to be done is to make a large working machine, and try it on a voyage."

"Quite so," he replied; "and I am prepared to

build one that will go to any part of the earth, or explore the higher regions of the atmosphere, or go down under the sea, or even make a trip to one of the nearer planets, Mars or Venus as the case may be. But I am poor; my little fortune is all but exhausted, and here, at the end of the race, within sight of the goal, I lack the wherewithal to reach it. Now, sir, if you can see your way to provide the funds, I will give you a share in the profits of the invention."

I pondered his words in silence. Visions of travel through the air in distant lands, above the rhododendron forests of the Himalayas, or the green Savannahs of the Orinoco, the coral isles of the Pacific; yea, further still, through the starlit crypts of space to other spheres were hovering in my fancy. The singular history of the man, too, had touched my feelings. Nevertheless, I hesitated to accept his offer there and then. It was hardly a proposal to decide upon without due consideration.

"I will think it over and let you know," said I at length. "Have you any objection to my consulting Professor Gazen, the well-known astronomer? He is a friend of mine. Perhaps he will be able to assist us."

"None whatever, so long as he keeps the affair

to himself. You can bring him to see the experiments if you like. All I reserve is that I shall not be asked to explain the inner action of the machine. That must remain a secret; but some day I hope to show you even that."

"Thanks."

CHAPTER IV.

THE ELECTRIC ORRERY.

"HALF-MOON Junction! Change here for Venus, Mercury, the Earth, Mars, Jupiter, Saturn, Uranus, Neptune!"

So I called in the style of a Clapham railway porter, as I entered the observatory of Professor Gazen on the following night.

"What is the matter?" said he with a smile. "Are you imitating the officials of the Universal Navigation Company in the distant future?"

"Not so distant as you may imagine," I responded significantly; and then I told him all that I had seen and heard of the new flying machine.

The professor listened with serious attention, but manifested neither astonishment nor scepticism.

"What do you think about it?" I asked. "What should I do in the case?"

"Well, I hardly know," he replied doubtfully.

"It is rather out of my line, and after my experience with Mars the other night, I am not inclined to dogmatise. At all events, I should like to see and try the machine before giving an opinion."

"I will arrange for that with the inventor."

"Possibly I can find out something about him from my American friends—if he is genuine. What's his name again?"

"Carmichael—Nasmyth Carmichael."

"Nasmyth Carmichael," repeated Gazen, musingly. "It seems to me I've heard the name somewhere. Yes, now I recollect. When I was a student at Cambridge, I remember reading a text-book on physics by Professor Nasmyth Carmichael, an American, and a capital book it was—beautifully simple, clear, and profound like Nature herself. Professors, as a rule, and especially professors of science, are not the best writers in the world. Pity they can't teach the economy of energy without wasting that of their readers. Carmichael's book was not a dead system of mathematics and figures, but rather a living tale, with illustrations drawn from every part of the world. I got far more help from it than the prescribed treatises, and the best of that was a liking for the subject. I believe I should have been plucked without it."

"The very man, no doubt."

"He was remarkably sane when he wrote that book, whatever he is now. As to his character, that is another question. Given a work of science, to find the character of the author. Problem."

"I shall proceed cautiously in the affair. Before I commit myself, I must be satisfied by inspection and trial that there is neither trickery nor self-delusion on his part. We can make some trial trips, and gain experience before we attempt to leave the world."

"If you take my advice you will keep to the earth altogether."

"Surely, if we can ascend into the higher regions of the atmosphere, we can traverse empty space. You would have me stop within sight of the goal. The end of travel is to reach the other planets."

"Why not say the fixed stars when you are about it?"

"That's impossible."

"On the contrary, with a vessel large enough to contain the necessaries of life, a select party of ladies and gentlemen might start for the Milky Way, and if all went right, their descendants would arrive there in the course of a few million years."

"Rather a long journey, I'm afraid."

"What would you have? A million years quotha! nay, not so much. It depends on the speed and the direction taken. If they were able to cover, say, the distance from Liverpool to New York in a tenth of a second, they would get to Alpha in the constellation Centaur, perhaps the nearest of the fixed stars, in twenty or thirty years—a mere bagatelle. But why should we stop there?" went on Gazen. "Why should we not build large vessels for the navigation of the ether—artificial planets in fact—and go cruising about in space, from universe to universe, on a celestial Cook's excursion—"

"We are doing that now, I believe."

"Yes, but in tow of the Sun. Not at our own sweet will, like gipsies in a caravan. Independent, free of rent and taxes, these hollow planetoids would serve for schools, hotels, dwelling-houses—"

"And lunatic asylums."

"They would relieve the surplus population of the globe," continued Gazen, warming to his theme. "It is an idea of the first political importance—especially to British statesmen. The Empire is only in its infancy. With a fleet of ethereal gunboats we might colonise the solar system, and annex the stars. What a stroke of business!"

"Another illusion gone," I observed "Think of Manchester cotton in the Pleiades! Of Scotch whiskey in Orion! However, I am afraid your policy would lead to international complications. The French would set up a claim for 'Ancient Lights.' The Germans would discover a nebulous Hinterland under their protection. The Americans would protest in the name of the Monroe Doctrine. It is necessary to be modest. Let us return to our muttons."

"Everybody will be able to pick a world that suits him," pursued Gazen, still on the trail of his thought. "If he grows tired of one he can look round for a better. Criminals will be weeded out and sent to Coventry, I mean transplanted into a worse. When a planet is dying of old age, the inhabitants will flit to another."

"Seriously, if Carmichael's machine turns out all right, will you join me in a trip?"

"Thanks, no. I believe I shall wait and see how you get on first."

"And where would you advise me to go, Mars or Venus?"

The professor smiled, but I was quite in earnest.

"Well," he replied, "Mars is evidently inhabited; but so is Venus, probably, and of the two I think you will find her the more hospitable and the nearest. When do you propose to start?"

"Perhaps within six months."

"We must consider their relative distances from

the earth. By the way, I don't think you have seen my new electrical orrery."

"An electrical orrery," I exclaimed. "Surely that is something new!"

"So far as I am aware; but you never know in these days. There is nothing new under the sun, or even above it."

So saying, he opened a small door in the side of the observatory, and, ushering me into a very dark apartment, closed it behind us.

"Follow me, there is no danger," said he, taking me by the arm, and guiding me for several paces into the darkness.

At length we halted, and I looked all around me, but was unable to perceive a single object.

"Where are we?" I enquired; "in the realms of Chaos and Old Night?"

"You are now in the centre of the Universe," replied Gazen; "or, to speak more correctly, at a point in space overlooking the solar system."

"Well, I can't see it," said I. "Have you got such a thing as a match about you?"

"Let there be light!" responded Gazen in a reverent manner, and instantly a soft, weird radiance was over all. The contrast of that sudden illumination with the preceding darkness was electrical in more senses than one, and I could not repress a cry of genuine admiration.

A kind of twilight still reigned, and after the first moment of surprise, I perceived that we were standing on a light metal gangway in the middle of a great hollow cell of a luminous black or dark blue colour, relieved by innumerable bright points, and resembling the night sky in miniature.

"I need hardly say that is a model of the celestial sphere," whispered Gazen, indicating the starry vault.

"It is a wonderful imitation," I responded, my awestruck eyes wandering over the mysterious tracts of the Milky Way and the familiar constellations of the mimic heavens. "May I ask how it is done—how you produce that impression of infinite distance?"

"By means of translucent shells illuminated from behind. The stars, of course, are electric lamps, and some of them, as you see, have a tinge of red or blue."

Most of the light, however, came from a brilliant globe of a bluish lustre, which appeared to occupy the centre of the crystal sphere, and was surrounded by a number of smaller and fainter orbs that shone by its reflected rays.

"This, again, is a model of the solar system," said Gazen. "The central luminary is, of course, the sun, and the others are the planets with their satellites."

"They seem to float in air."

"That is because their supports are invisible, or nearly so. Both their lights and periodic motions are produced by the electric current."

"Surely they are not moving now?"

"Oh, yes, and with velocities proportionate to those of the real bodies; but you know that whilst the actual movements of the sun and planets are so rapid, the dimensions of the system are so vast that if you could survey the whole from a standpoint in space, as we are supposed to do, it would appear at rest. Let us look at them a little closer."

I followed Gazen along the gangway which encircled the orrery, and allowed us to survey each of the planets closer at hand.

"This kind of place would make a good theatre for a class in astronomy," said I, "or for the meetings of the Interplanetary Congress of Astronomers, in the year 2000. You can turn on the stars and planets when you please. I wish you would give me a lecture on the subject now. My knowledge is a little the worse for wear, and a man ought to know something of the worlds around him—especially if he intends to visit them."

"I should only bore you with an old story."

"Not at all. You cannot be too simple and

elementary. Regard me as a small boy in the stage of

> "'Twinkle, twinkle, little star,
> How I wonder what you are!'"

"Very well, my little man, have you any idea how many stars you can see on a clear night?"

"Billions."

"No, Tommy. You are wrong, my dear boy. Go to the foot of your class. With the naked eye we can only distinguish three or four thousand, but with the telescope we are able to count at least fifty millions. They are thickest in the Milky Way, which, as you can see, runs all round the heavens, over your head, and under your feet, like an irregular tract of hazy light, a girdle of stars in short. Of course we cannot tell how many more there are beyond the range of vision, or what other galaxies may be scattered in the depths of space. The stars are suns, larger or smaller than our own, and of various colours—white, blue, yellow, green, and red. Some are single, but others are held together in pairs or groups by the force of gravitation. From their immense distance they appear fixed to us, but in reality they are flying in all directions at enormous velocities. Alpha, of the constellation Cygnus, for example, is coming towards us at a speed of 500 million leagues per annum, and some move a great deal faster. Most of them probably have planets circling round them in different stages of growth, but these are invisible to us. Here and there amongst them we find luminous patches or 'nebulæ,' which prove to be either clusters of stars or stupendous clouds of glowing gases. Our sun is a solitary blue star on the verge of the Milky Way, 20 billion miles from Alpha Centauri his next-door neighbour. He is travelling in a straight line towards the constellation Hercules at the rate of 20,000 miles an hour, much quicker than a rifle bullet; and, nevertheless, he will take more than a million years to cover the distance. Eight large or major planets, with their satellites, and a flock of minor planets or planetoids, are revolving round him as their common centre and luminary at various distances, but all in the same direction. The orbits, or paths, about the sun are ovals or ellipses, almost circular, of which the sun occupies one focus, and they are so nearly in one plane, or at one level, that if seen from the sun, they would appear to wander along a narrow belt of the heavens, called the zodiac, which extends a few degrees on each side of the Elliptic or apparent course of the sun against the stars. The planets are all globes, more or less flat at the poles, like an orange, and each is turning and swaying on its axis, thus exposing every part to the light and warmth of the sun. They are divided by the planetoids into an inner and an outer band. The inner four are Mercury, Venus, the Earth, and Mars ; the outer four are Jupiter, Saturn, Uranus, and Neptune. Moreover, a number of comets and swarms of meteoric stones or meteorites are circulating round the sun in eccentric paths, which cross those of the planets. Such is the solar system—a lonely archipelago in the ethereal ocean—a little family of worlds."

"Not without its jars, I'm afraid."

"The sun is chief of the clan," continued Gazen, "and keeps it together by the mysterious tie of gravitation. While flying through space, he turns round his own axis like a rifle bullet in 25 or 26 days. His diameter is 860,000 miles, and although he is not much denser than sea-water, his mass is over 700 times greater than the combined mass of all his retinue. Gravity on his surface being 28 times stronger than on the earth, a piece of timber would be as heavy as gold there, and a stone let fall would drop 460 feet the first second instead of 16 feet as here. He is built of the same kind of matter as the earth and other planets, but is hotter than the hottest electric arc or reverberatory furnace.

Apparently his glowing bulk is made up of several concentric shells like an onion. First there is a kernel or liquid nucleus, probably as dense as pitch. Above it is the photosphere, the part we usually see, a jacket of incandescent clouds, or vapours, which in the telescope is seen to resemble 'willow leaves,' or 'rice grains in a plate of soup,' and in the spectroscope to reveal the rays of iron manganese, or other heavy elements. What we call 'faculæ' (or little torches), are brighter streaks, not unlike some kinds of coral. The 'Sunspots' are immense gaps or holes in the photosphere, some of them 150,000 miles in diameter, which afford us a peep at the glowing interior. There are different theories as to their nature, hence they provide rival astronomers with an excellent opportunity of spotting each other's reputations. For instance, I look upon them as eruptions, and Professor Sylvanus Pettifer Possil (my pet aversion) regards them as cyclonic storms; consequently we never lose an opportunity of erupting and storming at each other. Above the photosphere comes a stratum of cooler vapours and gases, namely, hydrogen and helium, a very light element recently found on the earth, along with argon, in the rare mineral cleveite. Tremendous jets of blazing hydrogen are seen to burst through the clouds of the photosphere, and play about in this higher region like the flames of a coal fire. These are the famous 'red flames' or 'prominences,' which are seen during a total eclipse as a ragged fringe of rosy fire about the black disc of the moon. Some of them rush through the chromosphere to a height of 80,000 miles in 15 minutes.

"Higher still is the 'corona,' an aureole of silvery beams visible in a total eclipse, and resembling the star of a decoration. The streamers have been traced for hundreds of thousands of miles beyond the solar disc. It appears to consist of meteoric stones, illuminated by the sunlight as well as of incandescent vapours of 'coronium,' a very light element unknown on the earth, and probably, too, of electrical discharges. The 'zodiacal light,' that silvery glow often seen in the west after sunset, or in the east before sunrise, may be a prolongation of it."

"I daresay these meteorites are swarming about the sun like midges about a lamp," said I.

"And just as eager to get burnt up," replied Gazen, with a smile. "Let us pass now to the planets. The little one next the sun is Mercury, who can be seen as a rosy-white star soon after sunset or before sunrise. He is about 36 million miles, more or less, from the sun; travels round his orbit in 88 days, the length of his year; and spins about his axis in 24 hours, making a day and night. His diameter is 3,000 miles, and his mass is nearly seven times that of an equal volume of water. The attraction of gravity on his surface is barely half that on the earth, and a man would feel very light there. Mercury seems to have a dense atmosphere, and probably high mountains, if not active volcanoes. The sunshine is from four to nine times stronger there than on the earth, and as summer and winter follow each other in six weeks, he is doubtless rather warm.

"Venus, the 'Shepherd's Star,' and the brightest object in the heavens after the moon, can sometimes be seen by day, and casts a distinct shadow at night. She is about 67 million miles from the sun, revolves round him in 225 days, and rotates on her axis in 23 to 24 hours, or as Schiaparelli believes, in 224 days. Her diameter is 7,600 miles, and her mass nearly five times that of an equal volume of water. Gravity is rather less there than it is here. Like Mercury, she appears to have a cloudy atmosphere, and very high mountains. On the whole she resembles the earth, but is, perhaps, a younger as well as a warmer planet.

"The green ball, next to Venus, is, I need hardly say, our own dear little world. Terra, or the earth, is 93 million miles from the sun, goes round him in 365 days, and turns on her axis in 24 hours less four minutes. Her diameter is 7,918 miles, and her density is 5·66 times that of water. She is attended by a single satellite, the moon, which revolves round her in 27·3 days, at a distance of 238,000 miles. The moon rotates on her axis in about the same time, and hence we can only see one side of her. She is 2,160 miles in diameter, but her mass is only one-eightieth that of the earth. A pound weight on the moon would scale six pounds on the earth. Having little or no atmosphere or water, she is apparently a dead world.

"The red planet beyond the earth is Mars, who appears in the sky as a ruddy gold or coppery star. He is 141 million miles from the sun, travels his orbit in 687 days, and wheels round his axis in 24 hours 37 minutes. His diameter is 4,200 miles, and his mass about one-ninth that of the earth. A body weighing two pounds on the earth would only make half a pound on Mars. As you know, his atmosphere is clear and thin, his surface flat, and subject to floods from the melting of the polar snows. Mars is evidently a colder and more aged planet than the earth.

"He is accompanied by two little moons, Phobos (Fear), which is from ten to forty miles in diameter, and revolves round him in 7 hours 39 minutes, at a distance of 6,000 miles, a fact unparalleled in astronomy; and Deimos (Rout), who completes a revolution in 30 hours 18 minutes, at a distance of 14,500 miles.

"About 400 planetoids have been discovered up to now, but we are always catching more of them. Medusa, the nearest, is 198 million miles, and Thule, the farthest, is 396 million miles from the sun. Vesta, the brightest and probably the largest, a pale yellow, or, as some say, bluish white orb, visible with the naked eye, is from 200 to 400 miles in diameter. It is impossible to say which is the smallest. Probably the mass of the whole is not greater than one quarter that of the earth.

"Jupiter, surnamed the 'giant planet,' who almost rivals Venus in her splendour, is 480 million miles from the sun; travels round his orbit in 12 years less 50 days; and is believed to whirl round his axis in 10 hours. His diameter is 85,000 miles, and his bulk is not only 1,200 times that of the earth, but exceeds that of all the other planets put together. Nevertheless, his mass is only 200 to 300 times that of the earth, for his density is not much greater than that of water. What we see is evidently his vaporous atmosphere, which is marked by coloured spots and bands or belts, probably caused by storms and currents, especially in the equatorial regions. Jupiter is thought to be self luminous, at least in parts, and is, perchance, a cooling star, not yet entirely crusted over.

"Four or five numbered satellites, about the size of our moon and upwards, are circulating round him in orbits from 2,000 to 1,000,000 miles distant in periods ranging from 11 hours to 16 days 18 hours.

"Saturn, the 'ringed planet,' who appears as a dull red star of the first magnitude, is the most interesting of all the planets. He is 884 million miles from the sun; his period of revolution is 29½ years, and he turns on his axis in 10 hours 14 minutes. His diameter is 75,000 miles, but his mass is only 94 times that of the earth, for he is lighter than pinewood. His atmosphere is marked with spots and belts, and on the whole his condition is like that of Jupiter.

"Two flat rings or hoops, divided by a dark space, encircle his ball in the plane of his equator. The inner ring is over 18,000 miles from the ball, and nearly 17,000 miles broad. The gap between is 1,750 miles wide, and the outer ring is over 10,000 miles broad. The rings are banded, bright or dark, and vary in thickness from 40 to 250 miles. They consist of innumerable small satellites and meteoric stones, travelling round the ball in rather more than ten hours, and are brightest in their densest parts. Of course they form a magnificent object in the night sky of the planet, and it may be that our own zodiacal light is the last vestige of a similar ring, and not an extension of the solar corona.

"Saturn has eight moons outside his rings, the nearest, Mimas, being 115,000, and the farthest, Japetus, 220,400 miles from his ball. With the exception of Japetus, they revolve round him in the plane of his rings, and when these are seen edgewise, appear to run along it like beads on a string.

"Uranus, the next planet visible, is a pale star of the sixth magnitude, 1,770 million miles from the sun, and completes his round in 84 years. His axis, differing from those of the foregoing planets, lies almost in the plane of his orbit, but we cannot speak as to his axial rotation. He is 31,000 miles in diameter, and somewhat heavier, bulk for bulk, than water. Four satellites revolve round him, the nearest, Ariel, being 103,500, and the farthest, Oberon, 347,500 miles distant. Unlike the orbits of the foregoing satellites, which are nearly in the same plane as the orbits of their primaries, those of the satellites of Uranus are almost perpendicular to his own. They are travelled in periods of two and a half to thirteen and a half days.

"Neptune, invisible to the naked eye, but seen as a pale blue star in the telescope, is 2,780 million miles from the sun, and makes a revolution in 165 years. His diameter is about 35,000 miles, and his density rather less than that of water.

"Neptune has one satellite, at a distance of 202,000 miles, which, like those of Uranus, revolves about its primary in an orbit at a considerable angle to his own in five days twenty-one hours. Both Neptune and Uranus are probably dying suns.

"Comets of unknown number travel in long elliptical or parabolic orbits round the sun at great velocities. They seem to consist partly of glowing vapours, especially hydrogen, and partly of meteoric stones. 'Shooting stars,' that is to say, stones which fall to the earth, are known to swarm in their wake, and are believed to be as plentiful in space as fishes in the sea."

"The trash or leavings of creation," said I reflectively.

"And the raw material, for nothing is lost," rejoined Gazen. "Now, in spite of all its diversity, there is a remarkable symmetry in the solar system. The planets are all moving round the sun in one direction along circular paths. As a rule each is nearly as far again from the sun as the next within it. Thus, if we take Mercury as $\frac{3}{4}$ inch from the sun, Venus is about $1\frac{1}{4}$ inches, the Earth $2\frac{1}{4}$, Mars 2, the planetoids $5\frac{1}{4}$, Jupiter $9\frac{3}{4}$, Saturn 14, Uranus 36, and Neptune 60 inches. On the same scale, by the way, Enckes' comet at Aphelion, its farthest distance from the sun, would be about 12 feet; Donatis almost a mile; and Alpha Centauri, a near star in the Milky Way, some ten miles.

"The stately march of the planets in their orbits becomes slower the farther they are from the sun. The velocity of Mercury in its orbit is thirty, that of Jupiter is eight, and that of Neptune is only three miles a second. On the other hand, the inner planets, as a rule, take some twenty-four hours, and the outer only ten hours to spin round their axis. The inner planets are small in comparison with the outer. If we represent the sun by a gourd, 20 inches in diameter, Mercury will seem a bilberry ($\frac{1}{10}$ inch) Venus, a white currant, the Earth a black currant ($\frac{1}{4}$ inch), Mars a red currant ($\frac{1}{8}$ inch), the planetoids as fine seed, Jupiter an orange or peach (2 inches), Saturn a nectarine or greengage (1 inch), Uranus a red cherry ($\frac{3}{4}$ inch), and Neptune a white cherry (barely 1 inch in diameter). By putting the sun and planets in a row, and drawing a contour of the whole, we obtain the figure of a dirk, a bodkin, or an Indian club, in which the sun stands for the knob (disproportionately big), the inner planets for the handle, and the outer for the blade or body. Again, the average density of the inner planets exceeds that of the outer by nearly five to one, but the mass of any planet is greater than the combined masses of all which are smaller than it. The inner planets derive all their light and heat from the sun, and have few or no satellites; whereas the outer, to all appearance, are secondary suns, and have their own retinue of worlds. On the similitude of a clan or house we may regard the inner planets as the immediate retainers of the chief, and the outer as the chieftains of their own septs or families.

"How do you account for the symmetrical arrangement?" I enquired.

"The origin of the solar system is, you know, a mystery," replied the astronomer. "According to the nebular hypothesis we may imagine that two or more dark suns, perhaps encircled with planets, have come into collision. Burst into atoms by the stupendous shock they would fill the surrounding region with a vast nebula of incandescent gases in a state of violent agitation. Its luminous fringes would fly immeasurably beyond the present orbit of Neptune, and then rush inwards to the centre, only to be driven outwards again. Surging out and in, the fluid mass would expand and contract alternately, until in course of ages the fiery tides would cease to ebb and flow. If the impact had been somewhat indirect it would rotate slowly on its axis, and under the influence of gravity and centrifugal force acquire a globular shape which would gradually flatten to a lenticular disc. As it cooled and shrank in volume it would whirl the faster round its axis, and grow the denser towards its heart. By and by, as the centrifugal force overcame gravity, the nebula would part, and the lighter outskirts would be shed one after another in concentric rings to mould the planets. The inner rings, being relatively small and heavy, would probably condense much sooner than the large, light, outer rings. The planetoids are apparently the rubbish of a ring which has failed to condense into one body, perhaps through its uniformity or thinness. The separation of so big a mass as Jupiter might well attenuate the border."

"If the planetoids were born of a single small ring, might not several planets be condensed from a large one?"

"I see nothing to hinder it. A large ring might split into smaller rings, or condense in several centres."

"Because it seems to me that might explain the distinction between the inner and the outer planets.

Perhaps the outer were first thrown off in one immense ring, and then the inner in a smaller ring. Before separation the nebula viewed edgewise might resemble your Indian club."

"A 'dumb-bell nebula,' like those we find in the heavens," observed Gazen. "Be that as it may, the rings would collect into balls, and some of these, especially the outer, would cast off rings which would condense into moons, always excepting the rings of Saturn, which, like the planetoids, are evidently a failure. The solar system would then appear as a group of suns, a cluster of stars. in short, a constellation. Each would be what we call a 'nebulous star,' not unlike the sun at present; that is to say, it would be surrounded by a glowing atmosphere of vapours, and perhaps meteoric matter. Under the action of gravity, centrifugal force, and tidal retardation, their orbits would become more circular, they would gradually move further apart, rotate more slowly on their axes, and assume the shapes they have now. In cooling down, new chemical compounds, and probably elements would be formed, since the so-called elements are perhaps mere combinations of a primordial substance which have been produced at various temperatures. The heavier elements, such as platinum, gold, and iron, would sink towards the core; and the lighter, such as carbon, silicon, oxygen, nitrogen, and hydrogen, would rise towards the surface. A crust would form, and portions of it breaking in or bursting out together with eruptions and floods of molten lava, would disturb the poise of the planet, and give rise to inequalities of surface, to continents, and mountains. When the crust was sufficiently stable, sound, and cool, the mists and clouds would condense into rivers, lakes, or seas, and the atmosphere would become clear. In due course life would make its appearance."

"Can you account for that mystery?"

"No. Science is bound in honour, no doubt, to explain all it can without calling in a special act of creation; but the origin of life and intelligence seems to go beyond it, so far. Spontaneous generation from dead matter is ruled out of court at present. We believe that life only proceeds from life. As for the hypothesis that meteoric stones, the 'moss-grown fragments of another world' may have brought life to the earth, I hardly know what to think of it."

"Has life ever been found on a meteoric stone?"

"Not that I know. Carbon, at all events in the state of graphite and diamond, has been got from them. They are generally a kind of slag, containing nodules or crystals of iron, nickle, and other metals, and look to me as if they had solidified from a liquid or vapour. Are they ruins of an earlier cosmos—the crumbs of an exploded world—matter ejected from the sun—the snow of a nebulous ring—frozen spray from the fiery surge of a nebula? we cannot tell; but, according to the meteoric as distinguished from the nebular hypothesis of the solar system, the sun, planets, and comets, as well as the stars and nebula were all generated by the clash of meteorites; and not as I have supposed, of dead globes."

"Which hypothesis do you believe?"

"There may be some truth in both," replied Gazen. "The two processes might even go on together. What if meteorites are simply frozen nebula? It is certain that the earth is still growing a little from the fall of meteoric stones, and that part of the sun's heat comes from meteoric fuel. Most of it, however, arises from the shrinkage of his bulk. Five or ten million years ago the sun was double the size he is now. Twenty or thirty million years ago he was rather a nebula than a sun. In five or ten million more he will probably be as Jupiter is now—a smoking cinder."

"And the earth—how long is it since she was crusted over?"

"Anything from ten to several hundred million

years. In that time the stratified rocks have been deposited under water, the land and sea have taken their present configurations; the atmosphere has been purified; plants and animals have spread all over the surface. Man has probably been from twenty to a hundred thousand years or more on the earth, but his civilization is a thing of yesterday."

"How long will the earth continue fit for life?"

"Perhaps five or ten million years. The entire solar system is gradually losing its internal heat, and must inevitably die of sheer inanition. The time is coming when the sun will drift through space, a black star in the midst of dead worlds. Perhaps the system will fall together, perhaps it will run against a star. In either case there would probably be a 'new heaven and a new earth.'"

"Born like a phœnix from the ashes of the old," said I, feeling the justice of the well-worn simile.

"I daresay the process goes on to all eternity."

"Like enough."

The sublime idea, with its prospect of the infinite, held us for a time in silence. At length my thoughts reverted to the original question which had been forgotten.

"Now, whether should I go to Mars or Venus?" I enquired, fixing my eyes on these planets and trying to estimate their relative distances from the earth.

Gazen made a mental computation, and replied with decision,

"Venus."

"All right," I responded. "Venus let it be."

CHAPTER V.

LEAVING THE EARTH.

"CHECK!"

I was playing a game of chess with an old acquaintance, Viscount ———, after dinner, one evening, in the luxurious smoking-room of a fashionable club in the West End of London.

Having got his queen into a very tight corner, I sipped a glass of wine, lit a Turkish cigarette, and leaned back in my chair with an agreeable sense of triumph.

My companion, on the other hand, puffed rapidly at his cigar, and took a long drink of hot whiskey and water, then fixed his attention on the board, and stroked his beard with an air of the deepest gravity. Had you only seen his face at that moment you would have supposed that all the care of a mighty empire weighed upon his shoulders. The countenance of a grand vizier, engaged in considering an ultimatum of Lord Salisbury, were frivolous in comparison.

There is little doubt that if Lord ——— had applied to the serious business of life as much earnest deliberation as he gave to the movement of a pawn, he would have made a very different figure in Society. But having been born without any effort of his own to all that most men covet—rank, wealth, and title—he showed a rare spirit of contentment, and did his best to make the world happier by enjoying himself.

As he was a very slow player, I began to think of a matter which lay nearer to my heart than the game, I mean the project of travelling to Venus. Tests of the new flying machine, by Professor Gazen and myself, as well as our enquiries into the character of Mr. Carmichael, having proved quite satisfactory, I had signed an agreement for the construction of an ethereal ship or car, equally capable of navigating the atmosphere to distant regions of the globe, and of traversing the immense reaches of empty space between the earth and the other members of the solar system.

As Miss Carmichael had determined to accompany her father, and assist him in his labours, it was built to carry three persons, with room to spare for another, and the trial trips, made secretly on foggy nights, had encouraged us to undertake the longer voyage into space. I am glad to say that Professor Gazen, having taken part in one of these, had got the better of his caution, and finally made up his mind to join the expedition.

I suspect that he was influenced in his decision by the heroic example of Miss Carmichael. At all events I know he tried very hard to dissuade her from going; but all his arguments could not shake her inflexible resolution, and truly, there was something sublime in the quiet fidelity of this young woman to her aged father which commanded our admiration.

At length, all preparations for the voyage were complete, and as we did not wish to excite any remark, it was arranged that we should start on the first night that was dark enough to conceal our movements.

While these thoughts were passing through my head, a footman, in plush, entered the smoking-room, and presented a telegram on a golden salver. Anticipating the contents, I tore it open, and read as follows:

"*We leave to-night. Come on at once.*—CARMICHAEL."

After writing a reply to the message, I turned to the Viscount, who had never raised his eyes from the board, and said,

"You had better give me the game."

He simply stared at me, and asked,

"Why?"

"Well, make it a draw."

"Oh, dear no. Let's play it out."

"I can't. I'm sorry to say I must leave you now. I have just received a telegram making an urgent appointment. When beauty calls ——"

"Oh!" replied his lordship, with an amiable smile. "In that case we'll finish it another time. I mean to win this game."

"It will take you all your time."

"I'll wager you ten to one—a thousand sovereigns to a hundred that I win."

It is not my habit to lay wagers; but I was anxious to be gone.

"All right," I responded with a laugh, as I went away. "Good-night!"

On arriving at Mr. Carmichael's cottage I found the rest of the party waiting for me. No time was lost in proceeding to the garden, where the car stood ready to mount into the air. All the lights were out, and in the darkness it might have been mistaken for a tubular boiler of a dumpy shape. It was built of aluminium steel, able to withstand the impact of a meteorite, and the interior was lined with caoutchouc, which is a non-conductor of heat, as well as air-proof. The foot or basement contained the driving mechanism, and a small cabin for Mr. Carmichael. The upper shell, or main body, of an oval contour, projected beyond the basement, and was surmounted by an observatory and conning tower. It was divided into several compartments, that in the middle being the saloon, or common chamber. At one end there was a berth for Miss Carmichael, and at the other one for Professor Gazen and myself, with a snug little smoking cell adjoining it. Every additional cubic inch was utilised for the storage of provisions, cooking utensils, arms, books, and scientific apparatus.

The vessel was entered by a door in the middle, and a railed gallery or deck ran round it outside. The interior was lighted by ports, or scuttles, of stout glass; but electricity was also at our service. Air constantly evaporating from the liquid state would fill the rooms, and could escape through vent holes in the walls. This artificial atmosphere was supplemented by a reserve fund of pure oxygen gas compressed in steel cylinders, and a quantity of chemicals for purifying the air. It need hardly be said that we did not burden the ship with unnecessary articles, and that every piece of furniture was of the lightest and most useful kind.

I think we all felt the solemnity of the moment as we stepped into the black hull which might prove our living coffin. No friends were by to sadden us with their parting; but the old earth had grown dearer to us now that we were about to leave it, perhaps for ever. Mr. Carmichael descended by the trap into the engine room, while we others stood on the landing beside the open door, mute and expectant.

Presently, a shudder of the vessel sent a strange thrill to our hearts, and almost before we knew it, we had left the ground.

"We're off!" ejaculated Gazen, and although a slight vibration was all the movement we could feel, we saw the earth sinking away from us. At first we rose very slowly, because the machine had to contend against the force of gravity; but as the weight of the car diminished the higher we ascended, our speed gradually augmented, and we knew that in the long run it would become prodigious. The night was moonless, and a thick mantle of clouds obscured the heavens; but the planet Venus was now an evening star, and after attaining a considerable height, we steered towards the west. Our course took us over the metropolis, which lay beneath us like a vast conflagration.

Far as the eye could see, myriads of lights

glimmered like watch fires through the murk of the dismal streets, growing thicker and thicker as we approached the heart of the city, and appearing to blend their lustres. Through the midst of the glittering expanse we could trace the black tide of the river, crossed by the sparkling lines of the bridges, and reflecting the red lanterns of the ships and barges. The principal squares and thoroughfares were picked out, with rows and clusters of gas and electric lamps, as with studs of gold and silver. The clock on the Houses of Parliament glowed like the full moon on a harvest night. Now and again the weird blaze of a furnace, or the shifting beam of an advertisement, attracted our attention. With indescribable emotion we hung over the immense panorama, and recognised the familiar streets and buildings—the Bank and Post Office, St. Paul's Cathedral and Newgate Prison, the Law Courts and Somerset House, the British Museum, the National Gallery of Arts, Trafalgar Square, and Buckingham Palace. We watched the busy multitudes swarming like ants in the glare of the pavements from the dreary slums and stalls of Whitechapel to the newspaper offices of Fleet Street; the shops and theatres of the Strand; the music halls and restaurants of Piccadilly Circus. A deep and continuous roar, a sound like that of the ocean ascended from the toiling millions below.

"Isn't it awful!" exclaimed Miss Carmichael, in a tone of reverence. "What a city! I seem to understand how an angel feels when he regards the world in space, or a God when He listens to the prayers of humanity."

"For my part," said Gazen, "I feel as though I were standing on my head."

By this time we had lost the sense of danger, and gathered confidence in our mode of travel.

"I fancy the clouds overhead are the real earth," explained the astronomer, "and that I'm looking down into the starry heavens, with its Milky Way. I say, though, isn't it jolly up here—soaring above all these moiling mannikins below—wasting their precious lives grubbing in the mire—dead to the glories of the universe—seeking happiness and finding misery. Ugh!—wish I had a packet of dynamite to drop amongst them and make them look up. Hallo!"

The earth had suddenly vanished from our sight.

CHAPTER VI.

IN SPACE.

WE had entered the clouds.

For half-an-hour we were muffled in a cold, damp mist, and total darkness, and had begun to think of going indoors when, all at once, the car burst into the pure and starlit region of the upper air.

A cry of joyous admiration escaped from us all.

The spectacle before us was indeed sublime.

The sky of a deep dark blue was hung with innumerable stars, which seemed to float in the limpid ether, and the rolling vapours through which we had passed were drawn like a sable curtain between us and the lower world. The stillness was so profound that we could hear the beating of our own hearts.

"How beautiful!" exclaimed Miss Carmichael, in a solemn whisper, as if she were afraid that angels might hear.

"There is Venus right ahead," cried the astronomer, but in a softer tone than usual, perhaps out of respect for the sovereign laws of the universe. "The course is clear now—we are fairly on the open sea—I mean the open ether. I must get out my telescope."

"The sky does not look sad here, as it always does on the earth—to me at least," whispered Miss Carmichael, after Gazen had left us alone. "I suppose that is because there is so much sadness around us and within us there."

"The atmosphere, too, is often very impure," I replied, also in a whisper.

"Up here I enjoy a sense of absolute peace and well-being, if not happiness," she murmured. "I feel raised above all the miseries of life—they appear to me so paltry and so vain."

"As when we reach a higher moral elevation," said I, drifting into a confidential mood, like passengers on the deck of a ship, under the mysterious glamour of the night-sky. "Such moments are too rare in life. Do you remember the lines of Shakespeare:—

"'Look, how the floor of heaven
Is thick inlaid with patines of bright gold:
There's not the smallest orb which thou behold'st,
But in his motion like an angel sings,

> Still quiring to the young-eyed cherubims:
> Such harmony is in immortal souls;
> But whilst this muddy vesture of decay
> Doth grossly close it in—we cannot hear it.'"

"True," responded Miss Carmichael, "and now I begin to feel like a disembodied spirit—a 'young-eyed cherubim.' I seem to belong already to a better planet. Should you not like to dwell here for ever, far away from the carking cares and troubles of the world?"

The unwonted sadness of her tone reminded me of her devoted life, and I turned towards her with new interest and sympathy. She was looking at the Evening Star, whose bright beam softened the irregularities of her profile, and made her almost beautiful.

"Yes," I answered, and the words "with you" formed themselves in my heart. I know not what folly I might have spoken had not the conversation been interrupted by Gazen, who called out in his unromantic style,

"I say, Miss Carmichael! Won't you come and take a look at Venus?"

She rose at once, and I followed her to the observatory.

The telescope was very powerful for its size, and showed the dusky night side of the planet against the brilliant crescent of the day like the "new moon in the arms of the old," or, as Miss Carmichael said, "like an amethyst in a silver clasp."

"Really, it is not unlike that," said Gazen, pleased with her feminine conceit. "If the instrument were stronger you would probably see the clasp go all round the dusky violet body like a bright ring, and probably, too, an ashen light within it, such as we see on the dark side of the moon. By-and-by, as we get nearer, we shall study the markings of the terminator, and a shallow notch that is just visible on the inner edge of the southern horn. Can you see it?"

"Yes, I think I can. What is it?" replied Miss Carmichael.

"Probably a vast crater, or else a range of high mountains intercepting the sunlight, and making a scallop in the border of the terminator. However, that is a secret for us to find out. We know very little of the planet Venus—not even the length of her day. Some think it is eight months long, others twenty-four hours. We shall see. I have begun to keep a record of our discoveries, and some day—when I return to town—I hope to read a paper on the subject before the most potent, grave, and learned Fellows of the Royal Astronomical Society—I rather think I shall surprise them—

I do not say startle—it is impossible to startle the Fellows of the Royal Astronomical Society—or even to astonish them—you might as well hope to tickle the Sphinx—but I fancy it will stir them up a little, especially my friend Professor Sylvanus Pettifer Possil. However, I must take care not to give them the slightest hint of what they are to expect beforehand, otherwise they will declare they knew all about it already."

"Has it struck you that up here the stars appear of different colours at various distances," said Miss Carmichael.

"Oh, yes," answered Gazen, "and in the pure atmosphere of the desert, or on the summit of high mountains, we notice a similar effect. The stars have been compared to the trees of a forest, in different stages of growth and decay. Some of them are growing in splendour, and others again are dying out. Arcturus, a red star, for example, is fast cooling to a cinder. Capella, over there, is a yellow star, like our own sun, and past his prime. Sirius, that brilliant white or bluish star, which flashes like a diamond in the south, is one of the fiercest. He is a double star, his companion being seven and himself thirteen times massier than the sun; but they are fifty times brighter, and a million times further off, that is to say, one hundred billion miles away. These double or twin stars are often very beautiful. The twins are of all colours, and generally match well with each other—for instance, purple and orange—green and orange—red and green—blue and pale green—white and ruby. One of the prettiest lies in the constellation Cygnus. I will show it to you."

"Oh, how lovely!" exclaimed Miss Carmichael, looking through the glass. "The bigger star is a golden or topaz yellow, and the smaller a light sapphire blue."

"Some of the star groups and nebulæ are just as pretty," observed Gazen, turning his telescope to another part of the heavens; "most of the stars are white, but there is a sprinkling of yellow, blue, and red amongst them—I mean, of course, to our view, for the absorption of our atmosphere alters the tint."

"Does that mean that there is more youth than age, more life than death, in the universe?" enquired Miss Carmichael.

"Not exactly," replied the astronomer. "There is apparently no lack of vigour in the Cosmos—no great sign of decrepitude; but we must remember that we see the younger and brighter stars better than the others, and for aught we know there are many dark suns or extinct stars, as well as planets and their satellites. I should not like to say that the population of space is going down; but on the whole it may be stationary. I wish I could show you the cluster in Toucan, a rosy star in a ring of white ones."

"Like a brooch of pearls," said Miss Carmichael.

"Yes—not unlike that," responded Gazen, evidently amused at her comparison. "But that constellation is in the Southern Hemisphere. However, here is the 'ring' or 'planetary' nebula in the Lyre."

"What a wonderful thing!" exclaimed Miss Carmichael, with her eye at the instrument. "It looks to me like a golden hoop, with diamond dust inside."

I do not know where Miss Carmichael got her knowledge of jewellery, for to all appearance she wore none.

"Or the cup of a flower," she added, raising her head.

"Poets have called the stars 'fleurs de ciel,'" said Gazen, shifting the telescope, "and if so, the nebula are the orchids; for they imitate crabs, birds, dumb-bells, spirals, and so forth. Take a look at this one, and tell us what you think of it."

"I see a cloud of silver light in the dark sky," said Miss Carmichael, after observing it.

"What does it resemble?"

"It's rather like a pansy—or ——"

"Anything else?"

"A human face!"

"Not far out," rejoined Gazen. "It is called the Devil Nebula!"

"And what is it?" enquired Miss Carmichael.

"It is a cluster of stars—a spawn of worlds, if I may use the expression," answered Gazen.

"And what are they made of? I know very little of astronomy."

"The same stuff as the earth—the same stuff as ourselves—hydrogen, iron, carbon, and other chemical elements. Just as all the books in the world are composed of the same letters, so all the celestial bodies are built of the same elements. Everything is everywhere ——"

Gazen was evidently in his own element, and began a long lecture on the constitution of the universe, which appeared to interest Miss Carmichael very much. Somehow it jarred upon me, and I retired to the little smoking-room, where I lit a cigar, and sat down beside the open scuttles to enjoy a quiet smoke.

"Why am I displeased with the lucubrations of the professor?" I said to myself. "Am I jealous of him because he has monopolised the attention of

Miss Carmichael? No, I think not. I confess to a certain interest in Miss Carmichael. I believe she is a noble girl, intelligent and affectionate, simple and true; with a touch of poetry in her nature which I had never suspected. She will make an excellent companion to the fortunate man who wins her. When I remember the hard life she has led so far, I confess I cannot help sympathising with her; but surely I am not in love?"

I regret to say that my friend the astronomer, with all his good qualities, was not quite free from the arrogance which leads some men of science to assume a proprietary right in the objects of their discovery. To hear him speak you would think he had created the stars, instead of explaining a secret of their constitution. However, I was used to that little failing in his manner. It was not that. No, it was chiefly the matter of his discourse which had been distasteful to me. The sight of that glorious firmament had filled me with a sentiment of awe and reverence to which his dry and brutal facts were a kind of desecration. Why should our sentiment so often shrink from knowledge? Are we afraid its purity may be contaminated and defiled? Why should science be so inimical to poetry? Is it because the reality is never equal to our dreams? There is more in this antipathy than the fear of disillusion and alloyment. Some of it arises from a difference in the attitude of the mind.

To the poet, nature is a living mystery. He does not seek to know what it is, or how it works. He allows it as a whole to impress itself on his entire soul, like the reflection in a mirror, and is content with the illusion, the effect. By its power and beauty it awakens ideas and sentiments within him. He does not even consider the part which his own mind plays, and as his fancy is quite free, he tends to personify inanimate things, as the ancients did the sun and moon.

To the man of science, on the other hand, nature is a molecular mechanism. He wishes to understand its construction, and mode of action. He enquires into its particular parts with his intellect, and tries to penetrate the illusion in order to lay bare its cause. Heedless of its power and beauty, he remains uninfluenced by sentiment, and mistrusting the part played by his own mind, he tends to destroy the habit of personification.

Hence that opposition between science and poetry which Coleridge pointed out. The spirit of poetry is driven away by the spirit of science, just as Eros fled before the curiosity of Psyche.

How can I enjoy the perfume of a rose if I am

thinking of its cellular tissue? I grow blind to the beauty of the Venus de Medicis when I measure its dimensions, or analyse its marble. What do I care for the drama if I am bent on going behind the scenes and examining the stage machinery? The telescope has banished Phœbus and Diana from our literature, and the spectroscope has vulgarised the stars.

Will science make an end of poetry as Renan and many others have thought? Surely not? Poetry is quite as natural and as needful to mankind as science. All men are poetical, as they are scientific, more or less.

It might even be argued that poetry is for the general, for the man as a man; while science is for the particular, for the man as a specialist; and that poetry is a higher and more essential boon than science, because it speaks to the heart, not merely to the head, and keeps alive the celestial as well as the terrestial portion of our nature.

Shall we prefer the cause to the effect, and the means to the end, or exalt the matter above the form, and the letter above the spirit? Does not the tissue exist for the sweetness of the rose, the marble for the beauty of the stature, and the mechanism for the illusion of the play? The "opposition" between science and poetry lies not in the object, but in our mode of regarding it. The scientific and the poetical spirit are complementary, as the inside to the outside of a garment, and if they seem to drive each other away it is because the mind cannot easily entertain and employ both together; but one is passive when the other is active.

Keats drank "confusion to Newton" for destroying the poetry of the rainbow by showing how the colours were elicited; but after all was Newton guilty? Why should a true knowledge of the cause destroy the poetry of an effect? Every effect must be produced somehow. The rainbow is not less beautiful in itself because I know that it is due to the refraction of light. The diamond loses none of its lustre although chemistry has proved it to be carbon; the heavens are still glorious even if the stars are red-hot balls.

But stones, carbon, and light are familiar commonplace things, and fraught with prosaic associations.

True, and yet natural things are noble in themselves, and only vulgar in our usage. It is for us to purify and raise our thoughts. Instead of losing our interest in the universe because it is all of the same stuff, we should rather wonder at the miracle which has formed so rich a variety out of a common element.

But the mystery is gone, and the feelings and fancies which arose from it.

In exchange for the mystery we have truth, which excites other emotions and ideas. Moreover, the mystery is only pushed further back. We cannot tell what the elements really are; they will never be more than symbols to us, and all nature at bottom will ever remain a mystery to us: an organised illusion. Think, too, of the innumerable worlds amongst the stars, and the eternity of the past and future. Whether we look into the depths of space beyond the reach of telescope and microscope, or backward and forward along the vistas of time, we shall find ourselves surrounded with an impenetrable mystery in which the imagination is free to rove.

Science, far from destroying, will foster and develop poetry. It is the part of the scientific to serve the poetical spirit by providing it with fresh matter. The poet will take the truth discovered by the man of science, and purify it from vulgar associations, or stamp it with a beautiful and ideal form.

Consider the vast horizons opened to the vision of the poet by the investigations of science and the doctrine of evolution. At present the spirit of science is perhaps more active than the spirit of poetry, but we are passing through an unsettled to a settled period. Tennyson was the voice of the transition ; but the singer of evolution is to come, and after him the poet of truth.

If we allowed the scientific to drive away the poetical spirit, we should have to go in quest of it again, as the forlorn Psyche went in search of Eros. It is necessary to the proper balance and harmony of our minds, to the purification of our feelings, and the right enjoyment of life. Poetry expresses the inmost soul of man, and science can never take its place. Religion apart, what does the present age of science need more than poetry? What would benefit a hard-headed, matter-of-fact man of science like Professor Gazen if not the arts of the sublime and beautiful—if not a poetical companion —such as Miss Carmichael ?

* * * * * *

Thus, after a long rambling meditation, I had come back to my bachelor friend and the fair American.

"Yes," thought I, rather uneasily, I must confess, for I could not disguise from myself the fact that I was taken with her, "Gazen and she are not an ill-matched pair by any means. They are alike in many respects, and a contrast in others. They have common ground in their love and aptitude for science; yet each has something which the other lacks. She has poetry and sentiment for instance, but he—well, I'm afraid that if he ever had any it has all evaporated by this time. On the other hand, she"—but it puzzled me to think of any good quality that Miss Carmichael did not possess, and I began to consider that she would be throwing herself away upon him. "They seem to get on well together, however—monstrously well. I wonder what star he is picking to pieces now?"

I listened for the sound of their voices, but not a murmur passed through the curtain which I had drawn across the entrance to the smoking cabin. Only a peculiar tremor from the mysterious engines broke the utter stillness. Was I growing deaf? I snapped my fingers to reassure myself, and the sound startled me like the crack of a pistol. Evidently my sense of hearing had become abnormally acute. My mind, too, was preternaturally clear, and the solitude became so irksome that I rose from my seat, and looked out of the scuttles to relieve the tension of my nerves.

Apparently we had reached a great height in the atmosphere, for the sky was a dead black, and the stars had ceased to twinkle. By the same illusion which lifts the horizon of the sea to the level of the spectator on a hillside, the sable cloud beneath was dished out, and the car seemed to float in the middle of an immense dark sphere, whose upper half was strewn with silver. Looking down into the dark gulf below, I could see a ruddy light streaming through a rift in the clouds. It was probably a last glimpse of London, or some neighbouring town; but soon the rolling vapours closed, and shut it out.

I now realised to the full that I was *nowhere*, or to speak more correctly, a wanderer in empty space—that I had left one world behind me and was travelling to another, like a disembodied spirit crossing the gloomy Styx. A strange serenity took possession of my soul, and all that had polluted or degraded it in the lower life seemed to fall away from it like the shadow of an evil dream.

In the depths of my heart I no longer felt sorry to quit the earth. It seemed to me now, a place where the loveliest things never come to birth, or die the soonest—where life itself hangs on a blind mischance, where true friendship is afraid to show its face, where pure love is unrequited or betrayed, and the noblest benefactors of their fellowmen have been reviled or done to death—a place which we regard as a heaven when we enter it, and a hell before we leave it. . . . No, I was not sorry to quit the earth.

And the beautiful planet, shining there so peacefully in the west, was it any better? At a like distance the earth would seem still fairer, and perhaps even now some wretch in Venus is asking himself a similar question. Is it not probable that just as all the worlds are made of the same materials, so the mixture of good and evil is much the same in all? I turned to the stars, where in all ages man has sought an answer to his riddles. The better land! Where is it? if not among the stars. I am now in the old heaven above the clouds. Does it lie *within* the visible universe, as it lies within the heart when peace and happiness are there?

In that pure ether the glory of the firmament was revealed to me as it had never been on the earth, where it is often veiled with clouds and mist, or marred by houses and surrounding objects—where the quietude of the mind is also apt to be disturbed by sordid and perplexing cares. Its awful sublimity overwhelmed my faculties, and its majesty inspired me with a kind of dread. In presence of these countless orbs my own nothingness came home to me, and a voice seemed to whisper in my ear,

> "Hush! What art thou? Be humble and revere."

After a while, I perceived a pure celestial radiance of a marvellous whiteness dawning in the east. By slow degrees it spread over the starlit sky, lightening its blackness to a deep Prussian blue, and lining the sable clouds on the horizon with silver. At length the round disc of the sun, whiter than the full moon, and intolerably bright, rose into view.

With the intention of rejoining Professor Gazen in the observatory, and seeing it through his telescope, I flung away my cigar, and stepped towards the door of the cabin; but ere I had gone two paces, I suddenly reeled and fell. At first I imagined that an accident had happened to the car, but soon realised that I myself was at fault. Dizzy and faint, with a bounding pulse, an aching head, and a panting chest, I raised myself with great difficulty into a seat, and tried to collect my thoughts. For the last quarter of an hour I had been aware of a growing uneasiness, but the spectacle of sunrise had entranced me, and I forgot it. Suspecting an attack of "mountain sickness" owing to the rarity of the atmosphere, I attempted to rise and close the scuttles, but found that I had lost all power in my lower limbs. The pain in my head increased, the palpitation of my heart grew more violent, my ears rang like a bell, and I literally gasped for breath. Moreover, I felt a peculiar dryness in my throat, and a disagreeable taste of blood in my mouth. What was to be done? I tried again to reach the door, but only to find that I could not even move my arms, let alone my feet. Nevertheless, I was singularly free from agitation or alarm, and my mind was just as clear as it is now. I reflected that as the car was ever rising into a rarer atmosphere, my only hope of salvation lay in calling for help, and that as the paralysis was gaining on my whole body, not a moment was to be lost. I shouted with all my strength; but beyond a sort of hiss, not a sound escaped my lips. The profound silence of the car now struck me in a new light. Had Gazen and Miss Carmichael not committed the same blunder, and suffered a like fate? Perhaps even Carmichael himself had been equally careless, and the flying machine, now masterless, was carrying us Heaven knows whither. Strange to say I entertained these sinister apprehensions without the least emotion. I had lost all feeling of pain or anxiety, and was perfectly tranquil and indifferent to anything that might happen. It is possible that with the paralysis of my powers to help myself, I was also relieved by nature from the fears of death. I began to think of the sensation which our mysterious disappearance would make in the newspapers, and of divers other matters, such as my own boyhood and my friends, when all at once my eyes grew dim—and I remembered nothing more.

CHAPTER VII.

ARRIVING IN VENUS.

"TRY to speak—there's a good fellow—open your eyes."

I heard the words as in a dream. I recognised the voice of Gazen, but it seemed to come from the far distance. Opening my eyes I found myself prostrate on the floor of the smoking room, with the professor and Miss Carmichael kneeling beside me. There was a look of great anxiety on their faces.

"I'm all right," said I feebly. "I'm so glad you are safe."

It appears that a short time before, Gazen had closed the scuttles of the observatory and returned with Miss Carmichael to the saloon, then, after calling to me without receiving any answer, had opened the door of the smoking-room and seen me lying in a dead faint. Luckily Miss Carmichael had acquired some knowledge of medicine, partly from her father, and without loss of time they applied themselves to bring me round by the method of artificial respiration employed in cases of drowning or lightning stroke.

It would be tedious to narrate all the particulars of our journey through the dark abyss, particularly as nothing very important befell us, and one day passed like another. Now and then a small meteoric stone struck the car and glanced off its rounded sides.

"Old Charon," as Gazen and I had nicknamed Carmichael, after the grim ferryman of the Styx, seldom forsook his engines, and Miss Carmichael spent a good deal of her time along with him. Occasionally she chatted with Gazen and myself in the saloon, or helped us to make scientific observations; but although neither of us openly confessed it, I think we both felt that she did not give us quite enough of her company. Her manner seemed to betray no preference for one or the other.

Did she, by her feminine instinct, perceive that we were both solicitous of her company, and was she afraid of exciting jealousy between us? In any case we were all the more glad to see her when she did join us. No doubt men in general, and professors in particular, are fond of communicating knowledge, but a great deal depends on the pupil; and certainly I was surprised to see how the hard and dry astronomer beamed with delight as he initiated this young lady into the mysteries of the apparatus, and what a deal of trouble he took to cram her lovely head with mathematics.

We noted the temperature of space as we darted onwards, and discovered that it contains a trace of gases lost from the atmospheres of the heavenly bodies. We also found there a sprinkling of minute organisms, which had probably strayed from some living world. Gazen suggested that these might sow the seeds of organic life in brand-new planets, ready for them, but perhaps that was only his scientific joke. The jokes of science are frequently so well disguised, that many people take them for earnest.

Gazen made numerous observations of the celestial bodies, more especially the sun, which now appeared as a globe of lilac fire in the centre of a silvery lustre, but I will leave him to publish his results in his own fashion. We may claim to have seen the South Pole, but, of course, at a distance too great for scientific purposes. Judging by its appearance, I should say it was surrounded by a frozen land. The earth, with its ruddy and green continents, delineated as on a map, or veiled in belted clouds, was a magnificent object for the telescope as it wheeled in the blue rays of the sun.

Hour after hour, with a kind of loving fascination, we watched it growing "fine by degrees and beautifully less," until at last it waned into a bright star.

Venus, on the other hand, waxed more and more brilliant until it rivalled the moon, and Mercury appeared as a rosy star not far from it.

We soon got accustomed to the funereal aspect of the sky, and the utter silence of space. Indeed, I was not so much impressed by the reality as I had been by the simulacrum in my dream of sunrise in the moon. When I looked at the weird radiance of the sun, however, I realised as I had never done before that he was only a star seen comparatively near, and that the earth was but his insignificant satellite. Moreover, when I gazed down into the yawning gulf, with its strange constellations so far *beneath* us, I felt to the full the awful loneliness of the universe; and how that all life and soul were confined to mere sunlit specks thinly scattered here and there in the blackness of eternal night.

Steering a calculated course by the stars, we reached the orbit of Venus, and travelled along it in advance of the planet with a velocity rather less than her own, so as to allow her to overtake us. Some notion of the eagerness with which we scanned her approach may be gathered by imagining the moon to fall towards the earth. Slowly and steadily the illuminated crescent of the planet grew in bulk and definition, until we could plainly distinguish all the features of her disc without the aid of glasses. For the most part she was wrapped in clouds, of a dazzling lustre at the equator, and duskier towards the poles. Here and there a gap in the vapour revealed the summit of a mountain range, or the dark surface of a plain or sea.

I need hardly say that none of us viewed the majestic approach of this new world, suspended in the ether, and visibly turning round its axis, without emotion. The boundary of day and night was fairly well marked, and I pictured to myself the wave of living creatures rising from their sleep to life and activity on one side, and going to sleep again on the other, as it crept slowly over the surface. To compare small things with great, the denizens of a planet reminded me of performers under the limelight of a darkened theatre:

"All the world's a stage!"

We amused ourselves with conjectures as to our probable fate on Venus, supposing we should arrive there safe and sound.

"I suppose the authorities will demand our passports," said I. "Perhaps we shall be tried and condemned to death for invading a friendly planet."

"It wouldn't surprise me in the least," said Gazen, "if they were to put us into their zoological gardens as a rare species of monkey."

"What a ridiculous idea!" exclaimed Miss Carmichael. "Now *I* feel sure they will pay us divine honours. Won't it be nice?"

"You will make a perfect divinity," rejoined the professor with consummate gallantry. "For my part I shall feel more at home in a menagerie."

Thus far we had not observed any signs of intelligent beings on the cloudy globe, and it was still doubtful whether we should not discover it to be a lifeless world.

Our track did not lie exactly on the orbit of the planet, but sufficiently beneath it to let her attraction pull the car up towards her Southern Pole as it passed above us; and by this course of action we trusted to enjoy a wider field of atmosphere to manœuvre in, and probably a safer descent into a cooler climate than we should have experienced in attempting to land on the equator.

By an illusion familiar in the case of railway trains, it seemed to us that the car was stationary, and the planet rushing towards us. On it came like a great shield of silver and ebony, eclipsing the stars and growing vaster every moment. Under the driving force of the engines and the gravity of the planet, our car was falling obliquely towards the orbit, like a small boat trying to cross the bows of an ironclad, and a collision seemed inevitable. Being on the sunward side we could see more and more of the illuminated crescent as it drew near, and were filled with amazement at the sublime spectacle afforded by the strange contrast between the purple splendour of the solar disc in the black abyss of ether and the pure white celestial radiance which was reflected from the atmosphere of the planet.

The climax of magnificence was reached when the approaching surface came so close as to appear concave, and our little ark floated above a hemisphere of dazzling brightness under a hemisphere of appalling darkness faintly relieved by the glimmer of stars and the purple glory of the sun.

Ere we could express our admiration, however,

we were startled by a magical transformation of the scene. The sky suddenly became blue, the stars vanished from sight, the sun changed to a golden lustre, and the broad day was all around us.

"Whatever has happened?" exclaimed Miss Carmichael between alarm and wonder.

"We have entered the atmosphere of Venus," responded Gazen with alacrity. "I wonder if it is breathable?"

So saying he opened one of the scuttles, and a whiff of fresh air blew into the car. Thrusting his nose out, he sniffed cautiously for a while and then drew several long breaths.

"It seems all right as regards quality," he remarked, "but there's too little body in it. We must wait until we get nearer the ground before we can go outside the car."

The pressure of the atmosphere as taken by an aneroid barometer confirmed his observation, but as we were ignorant of its average density it could not give us any certain indication of our height. Far beneath us an ideal world of clouds hid the surface from our view. We seemed to be floating above a range of snowy Alps, their dusky valleys filled with glaciers, and their sovereign peaks glittering in the sun like diamonds. As we descended in a long slant, their dazzling summits rose to meet us, and the infinite play of light and shade became more and more beautiful. The gliding car threw a distinct shadow which travelled along the white screen, and equally to our surprise and delight became fringed with coloured circles resembling rainbows.

"It is a good omen!" cried Miss Carmichael.

"Humph!" responded the professor, shaking his head but smiling good-humouredly; "that is a mere superstition I'm afraid. It is simply an optical effect, a variety of the phenomenon called 'anthelia,' like Ulloa's Circle and the famous 'Spectre of the Brocken.'"

"Explain it how you will," rejoined Miss Carmichael, "to me it is an emblem of hope. It cheers my heart."

"I am very glad to hear it, and I should be very sorry to crush your hopes," said Gazen pleasantly. "We can sometimes derive moral encouragement and profit from external phenomena. A rainbow in the midst of a storm is a cheering sight. I daresay there is a reasonable basis, too, for certain superstitions. St. Elmo's Fire may, for instance, from natural causes, be a sign of good weather, only there is nothing supernatural about it."

"I am not in the secrets of the supernatural,"

replied Miss Carmichael, "but I believe that if we do not look for the supernatural, if we shut our eyes to it, we are not likely to see it."

"Science has proved that so many things formerly thought to be supernatural are quite natural," observed the astronomer a little more humbly.

"Perhaps the natural and the supernatural are one," said Miss Carmichael. "Does a thing cease to be supernatural because we know something about it?"

"Well, it may have another meaning for us. Before the days of science, great mistakes were made in our interpretations of phenomena. Superstition is born of ignorance, and we can see the germ of it in the child who is frightened by a bogie, or the horse that shies at the moonlight."

"It's higher parent is a belief in the unseen."

"In any case it has done an immense amount of harm," said the professor.

"And probably quite as much good," responded Miss Carmichael. "However, don't think me a friend of superstition. But in getting rid of it let us take care that we do not fall into the opposite error. It seems to me that if science had all its own way it would reduce man and nature to a little machine working in the corner of a big one; but I think it will cost us too dear if it make us lose our sense of the divine origin and spiritual significance of the universe."

Further argument was cut short by the car suddenly dashing into the clouds with a noiseless ease that astonished us, for they had appeared as solid as the rock.

Lost in the vapours, our car seemed at rest; but although we saw nothing, we could hear a vague and distant murmur which charmed our ears after the long silence of space like a strain of music. Whether this was due to the sounds of the surface collected in the clouds, or to electrical discharges I cannot say, for we were trying to solve the mystery by hearkening to it, when it abruptly died away as the car shot into the clear air beneath the clouds.

"The sea! the sea!" cried Miss Carmichael, starting up in joyful excitement to join her father; and sure enough we were flying above a dark blue hemisphere which could only be the ocean.

Gazen now made another test of the atmosphere, and, finding it satisfactory, we opened the door of the car and ventured on the gallery.

After our confinement the fresh air acted like a charm. It felt so cool and sweet in the nostrils that every breath was a pleasure. We inhaled it in long, deep, loving draughts, which imparted vigour to our exhausted frames, and intoxicated our spirits like laughing gas. I could hardly restrain a wild impulse to leap from the car into the unruffled bosom of the sea below, and Gazen, habitually staid, actually shouted with glee. His voice startled the utter stillness, and was mocked by a faint echo from the surface of the water. By timing the interval between a call and its echo we found it nearly ten seconds, which corresponded to a height of about a mile. A repetition of the test from time to time showed that the car was now travelling at a fairly constant level. The wide ocean spread all around us; neither sail nor shore, nor living creature was visible, and we had begun to ask ourselves whether we had not found a watery planet, when Gazen suddenly cried out,

"Land!"

"Whereaway?" I enquired with breathless interest.

He pointed a little to the right of our course, and following the direction of his finger, I saw a dim outline where sea and sky met. It might have been mistaken for the tip of a cloud, but as we advanced it rose above the horizon and took a definite shape not unlike a truncated cone.

The glasses showed it to be an island apparently of volcanic formation, and after a brief consultation with Carmichael, we steered towards it. The emotion of Columbus when he arrived at the Bahamas affords, perhaps, the nearest parallel to our feelings, but in our case the land in sight was the outlier of another planet. Watchful curiosity and silent expectation, the ineffable sorcery of new scenes, the mystery of the unknown, the romance of adventure, the exultation of triumph, and the dread of disaster, were inextricably blended in our hearts. It was a glorious hour, and come what might, we all felt that we had not lived in vain.

The island rose out of the sea like a volcanic peak, and was evidently encircled with a barrier reef, as we could trace a line of snowy surf breaking on its outer verge, and parting the sapphire blue of the deep water without from the emerald green shoals within. The coast, sweeping in beautiful bays, dotted with overgrown islets, and fended by rocky promontories, was rimmed with beaches of yellow sand. The steep sides of the mountain, broken with precipices, and shaggy with vegetation, ascended from a multitude of spurs and buttresses, resembling billows of verdure, and towered into the clouds.

I have used the word verdure, but it is really a misnomer, for although the prevailing tint of the foliage was a dark green, the entire forest was streaked like a rainbow with innumerable flowers, and the breeze which blew from it was laden with the most delightful perfume. Evidently it was all a howling wilderness, for we could not detect the slightest vestige of human dwellings or cultivation. We did not even observe any signs of bird or beast. A profound stillness brooded over the solitude, and was scarcely broken by the drowsy murmur of distant waterfalls.

A forest, like the sea or desert, has a magical power to stimulate the fancy and touch the primitive chords of the heart. Even a Scotch hillside, or a Devonshire moor, can throw their wild spells over the civilised man of letters, and appeal to savage or poetical instincts underlying all his culture. So now, where everything seen or unseen, was new and strange, and the imagination was quite free to rove, the charm was more intense. We stood and gazed upon the moving panorama like persons in a trance. The trees and plants grew in zones according to their different levels above the sea, after the manner of those on the earth, but we were too high to distinguish the various kinds. Apparently, however, feathery palms and gigantic grasses prevailed in the lower, and glossy evergreens, resembling the magnolia and rhododendron, in the middle grounds. All this part of the forest was so thickly encumbered with flowering creepers and parasites as to seem one immense bower, dense enough to exclude the sunlight and make a perpetual twilight underneath. The higher slopes were clad with pine-trees, having long thin needles, which hung from their boughs like fringes of green hair, and bushy shrubs which reminded me of heaths. Above these, enormous ferns with fronds twenty or thirty feet in length, and thickets draped in variegated mosses were thriving in the spray of a thousand slender cataracts which poured from the brink of the precipitous crags on the summit of the mountain.

Seen from a distance, the cliffs appeared of a ruddy tint, but on coming closer we found this was due to myriads of huge lichens of a deep crimson and orange, and that the natural colours of the rock, vermilion and blue, lemon, yellow, purple, and olive green, almost vied with those of the forest lower down the steep.

We glided over the crest at a point where it was almost free of cloud, and were astonished to find it carved by the weather into the most fantastic shapes, rudely imitating the colossal figures of men and animals, or the towers and turrets of ruined castles. After the novelty of this goblin architecture had passed, however, its effect was somewhat dreary. The wind, moaning through the lifeless aisles and crannies of the dripping rocks, the rolling mist and shuddering pools of water, induced a sense of loneliness and depression. The revulsion in our feelings was therefore all the greater when the car suddenly escaped from this height of desolation, and a magnificent prospect burst upon our view.

An immense valley seemed to lie far beneath us, but it was really a table-land of hills, rocks, and mountains, shaggy with vegetation, and flung together in riotous confusion like the billows of a raging sea. The stupendous cliffs behind us dropped sheerly down to the level of the plateau, some ten or twenty thousand feet below, and swept around it as a curving wall on either hand until they vanished in the distance. It was evidently the crater of the extinct volcano.

Our journey across that blooming wilderness will never fade from my recollection, but when I attempt to give the reader an idea of it, impressions crowd so thick and fast upon me as to choke my utterance; I am equally in danger of soaring into a wild extravagance of generality and sinking into a mere catalogue of detail. Yet I find it impossible to hit a mean that can do any justice to it. The extraordinary way in which the ancient lavas of the interior had been riven, upheaved, and piled upon each other by the volcanic forces, the bewildering variety and exuberance of the tropical plants and trees which battened on the rich and crumbling soil, completely baffles all description. What the imagination is unable to conceive, and the eye itself is overpowered in beholding, the pen can never hope to depict. Let the grandest mountain scenes of your memory be jumbled together as in a dream and overgrown with the maddest jungles of the Ganges or the Amazon, and the phantasmagoria would still be nothing to the living reality.

Most of the highest peaks and ridges, as well as the deepest valleys and ravines, were covered with the embowering forest; but here and there a huge boss of granite or porphyry reared its bare scalp out of the verdure like the head and shoulders of some antediluvian monster. The gigantic palms and foliage trees, all tufted with air-plants or strangled with climbers, were literally buried in flowers of every hue, and the crown of the forest rolled under us like a sea of blossoms. Every moment one enchanting prospect after another opened to our wondering eyes. Now it was a waterfall, gleaming like a vein of silver on the brow of a lofty precipice, and descending into a lakelet bordered with red, blue, and yellow lilies. Again it was a natural bridge, spanning a deep chasm or tunnel in the rock, through which a river boiled and roared in a series of cascades and rapids. Ever and anon we passed over glades and prairies, carpeted with orchids, and dotted with clumps of shrubbery, a mass of golden bloom, or tremendous blocks of basalt hung with crimson creepers. Butterflies with azure wings of a surprising spread and lustre, alighted on the flowers, and great birds of resplendent plumage flashed from grove to grove. A sun, twice the diameter of ours, blazed in the northern sky, but the intensity of his rays was tempered by a thin veil of cloud. The atmosphere although warm and moist, was not oppressive like that of a forcing-house, and the breeze was balmy with delicious perfume.

As each new marvel came in sight, unstaled by familiar and untarnished by vulgar associations, fresh from the hand of nature, so to speak, we were filled as we had never been before with an intoxicating sense of the divine mystery and miracle of life. For myself I was fairly dumbfounded with amazement, and my companion, the hard-headed sceptical astronomer, kept on crying and muttering to himself, "My God! my God!" as if he had become a drivelling fool.

We travelled league after league of this paradise run wild (I cannot tell how many) without noticing any change in the character of the scenery. At length, however, it grew less savage by degrees, and we entered on a park-like country which gained in loveliness what it lost in grandeur. Low hills, clad from base to summit in masses of gorgeous bloom, and mirrored in sequestered lakes fringed with pied water-lilies; groves of majestic cedars inviting to repose; rambling shrubberies and evergreen trees festooned with flowering vines; brooks as clear as crystal, murmuring over their pebbly beds, now hiding under drooping boughs, now lost in brakes of tall reeds and foliage plants; grassy meadows gay with crocusses, hyacinths, and tulips, or such-like flowers; isolated rocks and boulders mantled with vivid moss and lichens; hot springs falling over basins and terraces of tinted alabaster; clustering palms and groups of spiry pine-trees; geysers throwing up columns of spray tinged with rainbows; all these and a thousand other features of the landscape which must be nameless passed before our view.

Again and again we startled some herd of wild

quadrupeds or flock of gaudy birds unknown to science. Legions of large and burnished insects, veritable living jewels, might be seen everywhere, and flaunting butterflies hovered about the car. So far we had not observed the least sign of human occupation, and yet, as Gazen remarked, the appearance of the country seemed to betray the influence of art. It had not the wild and wasteful luxuriance of the earlier tract, of a region left entirely in the hands of Nature, but rather of a paradise which had been dressed and kept by the gods.

Owing to the height at which we were travelling, and the undulating character of the surface, we could not see very far ahead. At length, however, on emerging from a gap in a range of hills, we came upon a vast plain or prairie stretching away into the distance, and there in the blue haze of the horizon we saw, or fancied we saw, the architecture and gardens of a great city, on the borders of a lake, and above the lake, suspended in mid-air, a spectral palace, glittering in the sunbeams.

We raised a shout of joy and triumph at this discovery.

"Stop a minute, though," said Gazen, and a shade of doubt passed over his face. "Perhaps it is only a mirage."

We levelled our glasses at the distant scene, and scanned it with palpitating hearts. We could discern the general shape, and even the details of many houses, and the roofs and minarets of the palace, which was evidently built on the top of an island in the midst of the lake.

"That is not a phantasm," said I at last; "it is a real city."

Gazen made no reply, but turned and silently shook me by the hand. The tears were standing in his eyes.

A delightful breeze, fragrant with innumerable flowers, mantled the long grass of the prairie which was threaded by a maze of silver streams, and diversified with bosky woodlands. Ere long we observed fantastic cottages and picturesque villas nestling in the coppices, and as may be imagined we were all on tip-toe with curiosity to catch a sight of their inhabitants. We were anxious to see whether they looked like human beings, and how they were disposed towards us.

For a long time we looked in vain, but at length we saw a figure moving across the prairie which turned out to be that of—a *man*. Yes, a man like ourselves, but well stricken in years, and to judge by his costume apparently a savage. His back was towards us, and as we floated past the professor shouted in a tone loud enough for him to hear,

"Good evening, sir."

The native started, and lifting his eyes to the car beheld it with astonishment and awe. He raised his hands in the air, then dropped them by his side, and sank upon his knees.

"That's a good sign," said Gazen with a grim smile. "I wonder if he understands English. Let's try him again," and he cried out, "What's the name of this place?" but the car was going rapidly, and if there was any response it was lost upon the wind.

As we approached the city, the cottages became thicker and thicker. They were of various sizes, and of a light fanciful design adapted to a warm climate. Each of them was surrounded by a grove or garden rich in flowers and fruit. There were grassy trails and roads from one to another, but we did not see any fields or fences, flocks or herds.

We also saw more and more of the inhabitants—men, women, and children. They were evidently a fine race, tall, handsome, and of white complexion; but the men in general were darker than the women. From their gay dresses, and the condition of the land, we had set them down for savages;

but on a nearer view, their lack of arms, the beauty of their homes, and their own graceful demeanour, obliged us to reconsider our opinion. When they first saw the car they did not fly in terror, or muster hastily in armed and yelling bands. Many of them ran and cried, it is true, but only to call their friends, and while some stood with bowed heads and upraised hands as the car floated by, others, like the old man, fell upon their knees as though in prayer.

It was getting late in the day, and the sun was now sloping to the crest of the mountain wall encircling the crater. Accordingly we held a consultation with Carmichael as to whether we should land there, or proceed to the city.

Carmichael thought we should go on.

"But," said Gazen, "would it not be safer to try the temper of the people first, here in the country?"

"These people are not savages," replied Carmichael. "They are civilised, or semi-civilised, else how could they have built so fine a city as that appears. If we should see any signs of hostility amongst them, however, the car is plated with metal and will protect us—we have arms and can defend ourselves—and, besides, we can rise again, and slip away from them."

We decided to advance, but Gazen and I took the precaution to belt on our revolvers.

The huge limb of the sun, red and glowing, sank to rest in a bed of purple clouds on the summit of the rosy precipice, and filled all the green plain with a rich amber light. The fantastic towers and trees of the distant city by the lake shone in his mellow lustre; the solitary island swam in a flood of gold, and the quaint edifice which crowned it blazed with insufferable splendour. As the eerie gloaming died in the west, and thin grey mists began to veil the outlandish scene, we realised to the full that we were all alone and friendless in an unknown world, and a deep sentiment of exile took possession of our souls.

The gloaming fell, and myriads of lights twinkled in the dusk, some flitting about like fireflies, others stationary, while a hum of many voices ascended to our ears. The lights showed us that we were gliding over the city, and the voices told us that our arrival was causing a great commotion. Presently we floated above a large open space or square, lit with coloured lanterns, and evidently adorned with trees, fountains, and statuary. Here a great number of people had assembled, and as they appeared quite orderly and peaceable, we determined to land. While the car descended cautiously, Gazen and I kept a sharp watch on the crowd, with our revolvers in our hands. Instead of anger and resistance, however, the natives only manifested friendly signs of welcome. They withdrew to a respectful distance, and, dropping on their knees, burst into a song or hymn of wonderful sweetness as the car touched the ground.

CHAPTER VIII.

THE CRATER LAND.

A MAN of dignified and venerable mien stepped from the crowd, and followed by a train of youths and maidens, each bearing a vase or a tray of fruit and flowers, came towards the car. While yet some ten or twelve paces distant he stopped, and saluted Gazen and myself by lifting his hands gracefully in the air, and bowing his head. After we had acknowledged his greeting with due respect, he addressed us, speaking fluently, and in a reverent, not to say a humble tone; but his words, being entirely strange to our ears, we could only shake our heads with a baffled smile, and reply in English that we did not understand. On this a look of doubt and wonder passed over his face, and pointing, first to the car, then to the sky, he seemed to enquire whether we had not dropped from the clouds. We nodded our assent, and the astronomer, indicating the Earth, which was now shining in the east as a beautiful green star, endeavoured to let him know by signs that we had come from there.

The countenance of our host seemed to brighten again, and, saluting us with a profound obeisance, he said a few words to the attendants, who advanced to the car, and sinking upon their knees proffered us their charming tribute.

"Good!" exclaimed Gazen, testifying his delight and manifesting his gratitude by an elaborate pantomime.

I am afraid his performance must have appeared slightly ludicrous to the Venusians, for one or two of the younger girls had some difficulty in keeping their gravity. On a hint from the Elder the young people retired to their places, leaving their offerings upon the ground.

"They don't intend to starve us at all events," muttered Gazen to me, in an undertone. "The very fragrance of these fruits entices a man to eat them; but will they agree with our stomachs? Notwithstanding my scientific curiosity, and my natural appetite, I am quite willing to let you and Carmichael try them first."

Having found the value of gestures in our intercourse, the Elder leaned his head on one hand, and pointed with the other to a large house at the upper end of the square. His meaning was plain; but as we had already made up our minds to stay in the car, at all events until we had looked about us, Gazen signified as much by energetic but indescribable actions, and further contrived to intimate that we were all thoroughly tired and worn out with our voyage.

The Senior politely took the hint, and repeating his courteous salute, withdrew from our presence, accompanied by his followers.

"I told you so!" cried Miss Carmichael, when Gazen and I re-entered the car. "They are treating us like superior beings."

"It shows their good sense," replied Gazen, and even as he spoke a strain of heavenly music rose from the assembled multitude, and gradually died away as they departed to their homes.

We could not sufficiently admire the beauty and fragrance of the flowers and fruit, or the exquisite workmanship of the vases they had brought. What struck us most was the lovely iridescence which they all displayed in different lights. The vases in particular seemed to be carved out of living opals, yet each was large enough to contain several pints of liquor. Miss Carmichael decorated the dinner-table with a selection from the trays, but although we found the fruits and beverages delicious to the taste, we prudently partook very sparingly of them.

After dinner we all went outside to enjoy the cool evening breeze, but without actually leaving the car. It was hardly dusk, only a kind of twilight or gloaming, and it did not seem to grow any darker. Yet innumerable fire-flies, bright as glow-lamps, and of every hue, were flashing like diamonds against the whispering foliage of the trees.

With the exception of an occasional group or a solitary who stopped awhile to look at the car and then passed on, the square was deserted ; but the dwellings around it were lighted up, and being of a very open construction, we could see into them, and hear the voices of the inmates feasting and making merry. Needless to say that everything we observed was interesting to us, for it was all strange ; but we were so much exhausted with excitement that we were fain to go to bed.

Next day the professor and I, obeying a common impulse of travellers, got up early and went forth to survey our new quarters. It was a splendid morning, the whole atmosphere steeped in sunshine, and musical with the songs of birds. The big sun was peeping over the distant wall of the crater, but we did not feel his rays uncomfortably hot. A sky of the loveliest azure was streaked with thin white clouds, drawn across it like muslin curtains, and a cooling breeze played gently upon the skin. The dewy air, so spring-like, fresh and sweet, was a positive pleasure to breathe, and we both felt the intoxication, the rapture of life, as we had never felt it since our boyhood. The grass underfoot was green as emerald, and soft as velvet; fountains were flashing in the sunshine, statues gleaming amongst the flowering trees, and birds of brilliant plumage glancing everywhere.

The square opened on the lake, and afforded us a magnificent view of the island. It was conical in shape, and the peak, no doubt, of an old volcanic vent. I should say it was at least a thousand feet in height; the sides were a veritable "hanging garden," wild and luxuriant; and the summit was crowned by a glittering mass of domes, minarets, and spires. Numbers of people, old and young, were bathing along the beach, and swimming, diving, and splashing each other in the water with innocent glee. Large birds, resembling swans, double the size of ours, and of pale blue, rose, yellow, and green, as well as white plumage, were floating in and out, and some of the children were riding on their backs. Fantastic boats, with carved and painted prows, might be seen crossing the lake in all directions, some under sail, and others with rowers, keeping stroke to the rhythm of their songs. The shores of the lake, sloping quietly to the waterside, were covered more or less thickly with the houses and gardens of the city, and far in the distance, perhaps fifty, perhaps a hundred miles away, the view was bounded by the dim and ruddy precipice of the crater wall.

Regaling our eyes on the beautiful prospect, and our lungs on the pure atmosphere, we wandered along the beach, ever and anon pausing to admire the strange forms and beautiful colouring of the shells and seaweeds, or to pick up a rare pebble, then shie it away again, little thinking that it might have been a ruby, sapphire, or topaz, worth a king's ransom on the earth. At length the way was barred by the mouth of a broad river, and after a refreshing plunge in the lake, we returned home to breakfast.

During our absence Carmichael had been visited by our venerable host of the evening, whose name was Dinus, and a young man called Otāré, who turned out to be his son. They had brought a fresh supply of dainties, and what was still more important, some pictorial dictionaries and drawings which would enable us to learn their language. As the structure of it was simple, and the vocabulary not very copious, and as we also enjoyed the tuition of the young man, who was devoted to our service, and conducted us in most of our walks abroad, at the end of a fortnight we could maintain a conversation with tolerable fluency.

In the meanwhile, and afterwards, we learned a good deal about the country, and the manners and customs of its inhabitants. Womla, or Woom-la, which means the "bowl" or hollow-land, is evidently the crater of an extinct volcano of enormous dimensions, such as are believed to exist upon the moon. It belongs to an archipelago of similar islands, which are widely scattered over a vast ocean in this part of Venus, but is, we were told, far distant from the nearest of them. The climate may be described as a perpetual spring and summer, with a sky nearly always serene, and of a beautiful azure blue, veiled with soft and fleecy clouds.

Thanks to the lofty walls of the crater, which penetrate the clouds and condense their moisture, the land is watered with many streams. These flow into the central lake, which discharges into the surrounding ocean by a rift or chasm in the mountain side. Moreover, there are frequent showers, and heavy dews by night, to refresh the surface of the ground. Thunderstorms occur on the tops of the mountain and in the open sea ; but very seldom within the enchanted girdle of the crater. The air is remarkably pure, sweet, and exhilarating, owing doubtless to the high percentage of oxygen it contains, and the absence of foreign matter, such as microbes, dust, and obnoxious fumes. In fact, we all felt a distinct improvement in our health and spirits, a kind of mental intoxication which was really more than a rejuvenescence. Nor was the heat very trying, even in the middle of the day, because although the sun was twice as large as on the earth, he did not rise far above the horizon, and cooling breezes blew from the chilled summit of the cliffs. The vegetation seems to go on budding, flowering, and fruiting perpetually, as in the Elysian Fields of Homer, where

> "Joys ever young, unmixed with pain or fear,
> Fill the wide circle of the eternal year :
> Stern winter smiles on that auspicious clime
> The fields are florid with unfading prime ;
> From the bleak Pole no winds inclement blow,
> Mould the round hail, or flake the fleecy snow ;
> But from the breezy deep the blessèd inhale,
> The fragrant murmurs of the western gale."

The mysterious behaviour of the sun was a great puzzle to our astronomer. I have said that he rose very little above the horizon, or in other words the lip of the crater, as might be expected from our high southern latitude; but we soon found that he always rose and sank at the same place. In the morning he peeped above the cliffs, and in the evening he dipped again behind them, leaving a twilight or gloaming (I can scarcely call it dusk), which continued throughout the night. From his fixity in azimuth, Gazen concluded that Schiaparelli, the famous Italian observer, was right in supposing that Venus takes as long to turn about her own axis as she does to go round the sun, and that as a consequence she always presents the same side to her luminary. All that we heard from the natives tended to confirm this view. They told us that far away to the east and west of Womla there was a desert land, covered with snow and ice, on which the sun never shone. We also gathered that the sun rises to a greater and lesser height above the cliffs alternately, thus producing a succession of warmer and cooler seasons; a fact which agrees with Schiaparelli's observation that the axis of the planet sways to and from the sun. Gazen was intensely delighted at this discovery, partly for its own sake, but mainly, I think, because it would afford him an opportunity of crushing the celebrated Pettifer Possil, his professional antagonist, who, it seems, is bitterly opposed to the doctrines of Schiaparelli. But why did the sun rise and set every fifteen hours or thereabout, and so make what I have called a "day" and "night"? Why did he not continue in the same spot, except for the slow change caused by the nutation or nodding of Venus? Gazen was much perplexed over this anomaly, and sought an explanation of it in the refraction of the atmosphere above the cliffs producing an apparent but not a real motion of the orb.

The territory of Womla may be divided into three zones, namely, a central plain under cultivation, a belt of undulating hills, kept as a park or pleasaunce, and a magnificent, nay, a sublime wilderness, next to the crater wall.

The natural wealth of the country is very great. Some of its productions resemble and others are different from those of the earth. We saw gold, silver, copper, tin, and iron, as well as metals which were quite new to us. Some of these had a purple, blue, or green colour, and emitted a most agreeable fragrance. There are granites and porphyries, marbles and petrifactions of the most exquisite grain or tints. Precious stones like the diamond, ruby, sapphire, topaz, emerald, garnet, opal, turquoise, and others familiar or unfamiliar to us, fairly abound, and can be picked up on the shores of the lake. I presume that many of them have been formed on a large scale in chasms of the rock by the volcanic fumes of the crater.

What struck us most of all, however, was the prevalence of phosphorescent minerals which absorbed the sunlight by day, and glimmered feebly in the dusk. Professor Gazen seems to think that the presence of snow and clouds, together with these phosphorescent bodies, may help to account for the mysterious luminosity on the dark side of Venus.

The vegetation is wonderfully rich, varied, and luxuriant. As a rule, the foliage is thick and glossy; but while it is green to blackness in some of the trees, it is parti-coloured or iridescent in others. Many of the flowers, too, are iridescent, or change their hues from hour to hour. The beauty and profusion of the flowers is beyond conception, and some of the loveliest grow on what I should take for palms, ferns, canes, and grasses. A distant forest or woodland rivals the splendid plumage of some tropical bird. We heard of "singing flowers," including a water-lily which bursts open with a musical note, and of many plants which are sensitive to heat as well as touch, and if Gazen be correct, to electricity and magnetism. We saw one in a house which was said to require a change of scene from time to time else it would languish and die.

The borders of the lakes and ponds teemed with corals, delicate seaweeds, and lovely shells. Innumerable fishes of gay and brilliant hues darted and burned in the water like broken rainbows.

Reptiles are not very common, at least, in the cultivated zone ; but we saw a few snakes, tortoises, and lizards, all brightly and harmoniously marked. One of the snakes was phosphorescent, and one of the lizards could sit up like a dog, or fly in the air like a swallow. The variety and beauty of the birds, as well as the charm of their song, exceed all description. Most of them have iridescent feathers, several are wingless, and one at least has teeth. The insects are a match for the birds in point of beauty, if not also in size and musical qualities. Many of them are luminescent, and omit steady or flashing lights of every tint all through the night.

There are few large quadrupeds in the country, and so far as we could learn none of these are predaceous. We saw an animal resembling a deer on one hand, and a tapir on the other, as well as a kind of toed horse or hipparion, and a number of domestic pets all strange to us.

The people, according to their tradition, came originally from a temperate land far across the ocean to the south-east, which is now a dark and frozen desert. They are a remarkably fine race, probably of mixed descent, for they found Womla inhabited, and their complexions vary from a dazzling blonde to an olive-green brunette. They are nearly all very handsome, both in face and figure, and I should say that many of them more than realise our ideals of beauty. As a rule, the countenances of the men are open, frank, and noble; those of the women are sweet, smiling, and serene. Free of care and trouble, or unaffected by it, mere existence is a pleasure to them, and not a few appear to live in a kind of rapture, such as I have seen in the eyes of a young artist on the earth while regarding a beautiful woman or a glorious landscape. Their attitudes and movements are full of dignity and grace. In fact, during my walks abroad, I frequently found myself admiring their natural groups, and fancying myself in ancient Greece, as depicted by our modern painters. Their style of beauty is not unlike that of the old Hellenes, but I doubt whether the delicacy and bloom of their skins has ever been matched on our planet except, perhaps, in a few favoured persons.

From some experiments made by Gazen, it would appear that while their senses of sight and touch are keener, their senses of hearing and also of heat are rather blunter than ours.

Partly owing to the genial climate, their love of beauty, and their easy existence, their dress is of a simple and graceful order. Many of their light robes and shining veils are woven from silky fibres which grow on the trees, and tinged with beautiful dyes. Bright, witty, and ingenious, as well as guileless, chaste, and happy, I can only compare them to grown-up children—but the children of a god-like race. Thanks to the purity of their blood, and the gentleness of their dispositions, together with their favourable circumstances, they live almost exempt from disease, or pain, or crime, and finally die in peace at the good old age of a hundred or a hundred and fifty years.

Their voices are so pleasing, and their language is so melodious that I enjoyed hearing their talk before I understood a word of it. Moreover, their delightful manners evince a rare delicacy of sentiment and appreciation of the beautiful in life. We foreigners must have been objects of the liveliest curiosity to them, yet they never showed it in their conduct; they never stared at us, or stopped to enquire about us, but courteously saluted us wherever we went, and left us to make ourselves at home. We never saw an ugly or unbecoming gesture, and we never heard a rude, unmannerly word all the time we stayed in Womla.

Some of their public buildings are magnificent; but most of their private houses are pretty one-storied cottages, each more or less isolated in a big garden, and beyond earshot of the rest. They are elegant, not to say fanciful constructions of stone and timber, generally of an oval shape, or at least with rounded outlines; but sometimes rambling, and varying much in detail. Everyone seems to follow his particular bent and taste in the fashion of his home. Many of them have balconies or verandahs, and also terraces on the roof, where the inmates can sit and enjoy the surrounding view. They are doorless, and the outer walls are usually open so that one may see inside; but in stormy weather they are closed by panels of wood, and a translucent mineral resembling glass. They are divided into rooms by mats and curtains, or partitions and screens of wood, which are sometimes decorated with paintings of inimitable beauty. The ceilings are usually of carved wood, and the floors inlaid with marbles, corals, and the richer stones. There are no stuffy carpets on the floors, or hangings on the walls to collect the dust. The light easy furniture is for the most part made of precious or fragrant woods of divers colours—red, black, yellow, blue, white, and green. At night the rooms are softly and agreeably lighted by phosphorescent tablets, or lamps of glow-worms and fire-flies in crystal vases.

The dishes and utensils not only serve but adorn the home. Most of the implements and fittings are made of coloured metals or alloys. Many of the cups and vessels are beautifully cut from shells and diamonds, rubies, or other precious stones. Statuary, manuscripts, and musical instruments, bespeak their taste and genius for the fine arts.

Their love of Nature is also shown in their gardens and pleasure grounds, which are stocked with the rarest flowers, fruits, and pet animals; such as bright fishes, luminous frogs and moths, singing birds, and so forth, none of which are captives in the strict sense of the word.

Members of one family live under the same roof, or at all events within the same ground. The father is head of the household, and the highest in authority. The mother is next, and the children follow in the order of their age. They hold that the proper place for the woman is between the man and the child, and that her nature, which partakes of both, fits her for it. On the rare occasions when authority needs to be exercised it is promptly obeyed. All the members of the family mix freely together in mutual confidence and love, with reverence, but not fear. They are very clean and dainty in their habits. To every house, either in an open court or in the garden, there is a bathing pond of running water, with a fountain playing in the middle, where they can bathe at any time without going to the lake.

They deem it not only gross to eat flesh or fish, but also barbarous, nay cruel, to enjoy and sustain their own lives through the suffering and death of other creatures. This feeling, or prejudice as some would call it, extends even to eggs. They live chiefly on fruits, nuts, edible flowers, grain, herbs, gums, and roots, which are in great profusion. I did not see any alcoholic, or at least intoxicating beverages amongst them. Their drink is water, either pure or else from mineral springs, and the delectable juices of certain fruits and plants. They eat together, chatting merrily the while, and afterwards recline on couches listening to some tale, or song, or piece of music, but taking care not to fall asleep, as they believe it is injurious.

They rejoice when a child is born, and cherish

it as the most holy gift. For the first eight or ten years of its life it is left as much as possible to the teaching of Nature, care being taken to guard it from serious harm. It is allowed to run wild about the gardens and fields, developing its bodily powers in play, and gaining a practical experience of the most elementary facts. After that it goes to school, at first for a short time, then, as it becomes used to the confinement and study, for a longer and longer period each day. Their end in education is to produce noble men and women; that is to say, physical, moral, and intellectual beauty by assisting the natural growth. They hold it a sin to falsify or distort the mind, as well as the soul or body of a child. They seem to be as careful to cultivate the genius and temperament as the heart and conscience. Their object is to train and form the pupil according to the intention of Nature without forcing him beyond his strength, or into an artificial mould. Studious to preserve the harmony and unity of mind, soul, and body, they never foster one to the detriment of the others, but seek to develop the whole person.

It is not so much words as things, not so much facts, dates, and figures, as principles, ideas, and sentiments, which they endeavour to teach. The scholar is made familiar with what he is told by observation and experience whenever it is possible, for that is how Nature teaches. Precept, they say, is good, and example is better; but an ideal of perfection is best of all.

At first more attention is paid to the cultivation of the body than the mind. Not only are the boys and girls trained in open-air gymnasia, or contend in games, but they also work in the gardens, and during the holidays are sent into the wilderness under the guidance of their elders, especially their elder brothers, to rough it there in primitive freedom.

The first lessons of the pupil are very short and simple, but as his mind ripens they become longer and more difficult. The education of the soul precedes that of the mind. They wish to make their children good before they make them clever; and good by the feelings of the heart rather than the instruction of the head. Every care is taken to refine and strengthen the sentiments and instincts, the conscience, good sense and taste, as well as the affections, filial piety, friendship, and the love of Nature. Spiritual and moral ideals are inculcated by means of innocent and simple tales or narratives. Children are taught to obey the authority placed over them, or in their own breast, and to sacrifice all to their duty. The conduct of the teacher must be irreproachable, because he is a model to them ; but while they look upon him as their friend and guide, he leaves them free to choose their own companions and amuse themselves in their own way.

In the cultivation of the mind they give the first and foremost place to the imagination. The reason, they say, is mechanical, and cannot rise above the known ; that is to say, the real ; whereas the imagination is creative and attains to the unknown, the ideal. Its highest work is the creation of beauty. Because it is unruly, and precarious in its action, however, the imagination requires the most careful guidance, and the assistance of the reason. Students are taught to idealise and invent, as well as to analyse and reason, but without disturbing the equilibrium of the faculties by acquiring a pronounced habit of one or the other. It is better, they say, to be reasonable than a reasoner ; to be imaginative than a dreamer ; and to have discernment or insight than mere knowledge.

The most important study of all is the art of living, or in other words the art of leading a simple, noble, and beautiful life. It finishes their education, and consists in the reduction of their highest precepts and ideals to practice. The reasons for every lesson are given so far as they are known, and they are always founded in the nature of things. A pupil is taught to act in a particular way, not in the hope of a reward or in the fear of punishment, but because it would be contrary to the laws of matter and spirit to act otherwise ; in short, because it is right. They hold that life is its own end as well as its own reward. According as it is good or bad, so it achieves or fails of its purpose, and is happy or miserable. We are happy by our emotions or feelings, and through these by our actions. Happiness comes from goodness, but is not perfect without health, beauty, and fitness: hence the pupils are taught self-regulation, practical hygiene, and a graceful manner. Indeed, their passion for beauty is such that they regard nothing as perfect until it is beautiful.

As beauty of mind, soul, and body, is their aim, a beautiful person is held in the highest honour. Prizes are offered for beauty, and statues are erected to the winners. Many are called after some particular trait; for example, "Timārē of the lovely toes," and a pretty eyelash is a title to public fame. Beauty they say is twice blessed, since it pleases the possessor as well as others.

The sense of existence, apart from what they do

or gain, is their chief happiness. Their "ealo," or the height of felicity, is a passive rather than an active state. It is (if I am not mistaken) a kind of serene rapture or tranquil ecstasy of the soul, which is born doubtless from a perfect harmony between the person and his environment. In it, they say, the illusion of the world is complete, and life is another name for music and love.

As far as I could learn, this condition, though independent of sexual love, is enhanced by it. On the one hand it is spoiled by too much thought, and on the other by too much passion. They cherish it as they cherish all the natural illusions (which are sacred in their eyes), but being a state of repose it is transient, and only to be enjoyed from time to time.

Since an unfit employment is a mistake, and a source of unhappiness, everyone is free to choose the work that suits his nature. Parents and teachers only help him to discover himself. One is called to his work by a love for it, and the pleasure he takes in doing it easily and well. If his bent is vague or tardy, he is allowed to change, and feel his way to it by trial. Since the work or vocation is not a means of living, there is no compulsion in it. Their aim is to do right in carrying out the true intentions of Nature.

For the same reason everyone is free to choose the partner of his life. They are monogamists, and believe that nothing can justify marriage but love on both sides. The rite is very simple, and consists in the elected pair sipping from the same dish of sacred water. It is called "drinking of the cup."

Most of them die gradually of old age, and they do not seem to share our fear and horror of death, but to regard it with a sad and pleasing melancholy. The body is reduced to ashes on a pyre of fragrant wood, and the songs they sing around it only breathe a tender regret for their loss, mingled with a joyful hope of meeting again. They neither preserve the dust as a memento, nor wear any kind of mourning; but they cherish the memory of the absent in their hearts.

They believe that labour like virtue is a necessity, and its own reward; but it is moderate labour of the right sort, which is a blessing and not a curse. They all seem happy at their work, which is often cheered by music, songs, or tales. Everyone enjoys his task, and tries to attain the perfection of skill and grace. Those who excel are honoured, and sometimes commemorated with statues.

They seem artists in all, and above all. They hold that every beautiful thing has a use, and they never make a useful thing without beauty. Apart from portraits, their pictures and statuary are mostly historical, or else ideal representations. Many of these are typical of life ; for example, a boy at play, a pair of lovers, a mother weaning her child, and the parting of friends. The ideal of art is to them not merely a show to please the eye for a while, but a model to be realised in their own lives ; and I daresay it has helped to make them such a fine people. They are clever architects and gardeners. Indeed, the whole country may be described as a vast ornamental garden. In the middle zone, which borders on the wilderness, their wonderful art of beautifying natural scenery is at its best. They have a good many simple machines and implements, but I should not call them a scientific people. Gazen, who enquired into the matter, was told by Otāré, himself an artist, by the way, that science in their opinion had a tendency to destroy the illusion of Nature and impair the finer sentiments and spontaneity of the soul ; hence they left the systematic study of it to the few who possess a decided bias for it. As a rule they are content to admire.

They have many books of various kinds, either printed or finely written and illustrated by hand. I should say their favourite reading was history and travels, or else poetry and fiction; anything having a human interest, more especially of a pathetic order. Everyone is taught to read aloud, and if he possess the voice and talent, to recite. Poets are highly esteemed, and not only read their poems to the people, but also teach elocution. They have dramatic performances on certain days, and seem to prefer tragedies or affecting plays, perhaps because these awaken feelings which their happy lot in general permits to sleep. They are very fond of music, and can all sing or play on some musical instrument. Their favourite melodies are mostly in a minor key, and they dislike noisy music; indeed, noise of any sort. Gesture and the dance are fine arts, and they can imitate almost any action without words. A favourite amusement is to gather in the dusk of the evening, crowned with flowers, or wearing fanciful dresses, and sing or dance together by the light of the fire-flies.

The inhabitants of the whole island live as one happy family. Recognising their kinship by intermarriage, and their isolation in the world, they never forget that the good or ill of a part is the good or ill of the whole, and their object is to secure the happiness of one and all. It is considered right to help another in trouble before thinking of oneself.

When Gazen explained the doctrine of "the struggle for existence ending in the survival of the fittest" to Otārē, he replied that it was an excellent principle for snakes; but he considered it beneath the dignity and wisdom of men to struggle for a life which could be maintained by the labour of love, and ought to be devoted to rational or spiritual enjoyment.

Thanks to the helpful spirit which animates them, and the bounty of Nature, nobody is ever in want. As a rule, the garden around each home provides for the family, and any surplus goes to the public stores, or rather free tables, where anyone takes what he may require.

As I have already hinted, personal merit of every kind is honoured amongst them.

Dinus, the gentleman who received us on the night of our arrival, is the chief man or head of the community, and was appointed to the post for his wisdom, character, and age. He is assisted in the government by a council of a hundred men, and there are district officers in various parts of the country.

They have no laws, or at all events their old laws have become a dead letter. Custom and public opinion take their place. Crime is practically unknown amongst them, and when a misdemeanour is committed the culprit is in general sufficiently punished by his own shame and remorse. However, they have certain humane penalties, such as fines or restitution of stolen goods; but they never resort to violence or take life, and only in extreme cases of depravity and madness do they infringe on the liberty of an individual.

Quarrels and sickness of mind or body are almost unknown amongst them. The care and cure of the person is a portion of the art of life as it is taught in the schools.

An account of this remarkable people would not be complete without some reference to their religion; but owing to their reticence on sacred subjects, and the shortness of our visit, I was unable to learn much about it. They believe, however, in a Supreme Being, whom they only name by epithets such as "The Giver" or "The Divine Artist." They also believe in the immortality of the soul. One of their proverbs, "Life is good, and good is life," implies that goodness means life, and badness death. They hold that every thought, word, and deed, is by the nature of things its own reward or punishment, here or hereafter. Their ideals of childlike innocence, and the reign of love, seem to be essentially Christian.

Their solicitude and kindness extends to all that lives and suffers, and they regard the world around them as a divine work which they are to reverence and perfect.

Our visit fell during a great religious festival and holiday, which they keep once a year, and by the courtesy of Dinus, or his son, we witnessed many of their sacred concerts, dances, games, and other celebrations. Of these, however, I shall only describe the principal ceremony, which is called "Plucking the Flower," and appears to symbolise the passage of the soul into a higher life.

CHAPTER IX.

THE FLOWER OF THE SOUL.

EARLY on the chief day of the festival Otāré came and took us to see the mystical rite of cutting the "Flower of the Soul."

The morning was fine, and the clear waters of the lake were bright with boats filled with joyous parties bound like ourselves for the Holy Island.

Landing at a noble quay of red granite, we climbed the steep and shaggy sides of the mountain by a sacred and winding avenue, bordered with blooming trees and statuary. Most of the figures were exquisitely carved in a white wood or stone, having a pearly sheen, and represented the former priestesses of the Temple, or illustrated the animating spirit of the cult.

On gaining the summit we found ourselves at the brim of a spacious hollow or basin, which in past ages must have been the crater of the volcanic peak. The grassy slopes of the basin were laid out in flower gardens and terraces of coloured marbles, shaded with sombre trees, and ornamented with sculpture. In the bottom lay an oval sheet of water a mile long or more, and from the midst of it, towards the near end, a beautiful islet, crowned by a magnificent temple, rose like a mirage to the view, and seemed to float on its glassy bosom.

Words of mine cannot give any idea of that sublime architecture, which resembled no earthly order, though it seemed to partake of both the Saracenic and the Indian. Fragrant timber, precious stones, and burnished metals; in fine, the richest materials known to the builders, had been united with consummate art into one harmonious emblem of their faith. The first beams of the rising sun blazed on its golden roof and fretted pinnacles of diamond, and ruby, sapphire, topaz, and emerald; but the lower part was still in shadow. Nevertheless, we could distinguish a grand portal in the southern front, which faced the sun, and a broad flight of marble steps descending from it into the water; but the massive doors were shut, and not a soul was to be seen about the temple.

As the worshippers arrived they seated themselves on the turf amongst the flowering shrubs, or on the benches along the terraces, and either spoke in subdued tones, or preserved a religious silence. Otāré led us to a kind of throne or stand facing the temple, and raised above the other seats, where his father, as chief of the community, sat in state. Dinus received us with his usual gracious dignity, and gave us chairs on his right and left hand.

From this height we enjoyed a splendid panorama of the Craterland, at least that portion which had already caught the sunshine. It lay beneath us like a picture, the surface rising in a series of zones from the central sea, which mirrored the serene azure and plume-like vapours of the heavens, through the sweet meadows, and the smiling gardens, to the luxuriant wilderness beyond; and we could plainly see the shadow of the bounding rampart shrink towards the south as the sun mounted higher and higher.

It was a lovely dawn. A rosy mist hung like a veil of gauze over the southern sky, and from behind a bar of purple cloud, lined with gold, which rested on the summit of the cliffs, a coronet of auroral beams or crepuscular rays, blue on a pink ground, shot upwards, heralding the advent of the sun, and reminding me of the ancient simile of the earth as a bride awaiting the arrival of her lord.

At length the first glowing tip of the solar disc peeped over the rim of the crater, and a deep low murmur, swelling to a shrill cry, ascended from the passive multitude.

All the people rose to their feet, and every eye was turned on the south front of the temple, which was now illuminated to the edge of the water. As the sunlight crept over the surface it sparkled on the dense foliage of what seemed a bed of water-lilies flourishing quite close to the marble stairs.

Presently a rich and stately barge, moved by crimson oars, and enlivened with young girls draped in sky-blue, was seen to glide round a corner of the temple, and come to rest beside the water-lilies.

A deep silence, as of breathless expectation, fell upon the vast assembly, and then, without other warning, the great purple doors of the temple swung open, and revealed a white-robed figure walking at the head of a glittering procession of maidens decked in jewels and luminous scarves, which vied with the colours of the rainbow. It was the young priestess and her train of virgins.

Simultaneously the immense multitude raised their voices in a sacred hymn of melting sweetness, very low at first, but gathering volume as the priestess descended the marble stairs to the water-side.

Here, on the lowest of the steps, one of her maidens put into her hand a sacred knife or sickle, which, as Otārê informed us had a blade of gold, and a handle of opal. The woman then retired, and we saw her stand erect for a moment in the full blaze of the mellow sunlight, with her golden hair falling about her in a kind of glory, and stretch out her arms towards the sun in a superb attitude of adoration. Then, with a slow and swan-like movement, she entered the water, and wading among the lilies, cut the sacred blossom, and held it aloft in triumph, while the music swelled to a mighty pæan of thanksgiving and praise.

After that she went on board the barge, which had been waiting for her, and was rowed around the border of the lake not far from the shore, so that the onlookers might see the loveliness of the flower, and even smell its perfume. The barge was not unlike an ancient galley in shape, but ornately curved like the proa of a South Sea Islander. The rowers were concealed underneath the deck, but the crimson oars kept time to the music of their voices, and the spectators joined in the song as the vessel glided onwards.

As for the priestess, she lay reclining under a golden canopy on the poop, with her face half turned towards the people, and holding the sacred lily in her hand, whilst two of her maidens fanned her with brilliant plumes,

> "And made their bends adorning."

Ever since she had come out of the temple I had scarcely taken my eyes off her, and now that I could see the marvellous beauty of her countenance, I was absolutely fascinated. Never shall I forget these moments as long as I live, and yet I cannot give a clear and connected relation of them. I see only a picture in my mind of a purple couch under a golden canopy, a fair form, a beautiful head crowned with golden hair, a glowing arm holding a white flower on its long green stalk. Suddenly, as if impelled by an instinct, she turns her face full upon me as the barge comes opposite to her father's throne. I see her great violet eyes fixed upon mine as though she would read into my very soul. I do not shrink from that pure search. On the contrary, I feel myself drawn towards her by an irresistible attraction, and return her gaze.

She does not look away. She smiles—yes, she smiles upon me, and inclines her head to see me, like a sunflower following the sun, as she is floating past.

From that moment I was an altered man. The vision of that peerless beauty had worked a miracle in my nature. A strange peace, an unfathomable joy, I should rather say an ecstacy of bliss, reigned in my heart. I felt that I had found something for which my soul had craved without knowing it, and had been seeking unawares—something beyond all price, which is not merely the best that life, eternity, can offer; but gives to life, eternity, an inestimable value—I felt that I had found the counterpart of myself—the celestial mate of my spirit. Henceforth there was only one woman in the world, in the universe, for me. A mysterious instinct whispered that we belonged to each other—that this incomparable creature was mine by an inviolable right, if not on this side of time at all events hereafter, and for ever. I felt, too, that my own being had now completed its development, and burst into bloom like a plant under the vivifying rays of the sun.

Exulting in my new-found happiness, and overcome with gratitude for it, I watched the receding boat in a sort of trance until the matter-of-fact voice of Gazen broke the spell.

"Prettiest sight I ever saw in my life," said he to Otāré. "Quite a living picture."

"I am glad you like it," responded Otāré evidently gratified.

"But what is the good of it?" enquired the professor.

"The good of it?" rejoined the Venusian; "it is beautiful, and gives us pleasure."

"Oh, of course; but what is the meaning—the inner meaning of it?"

"Ah! the meaning of it," said Otārė, a new light breaking on him, "I will explain. You saw the flower which the priestess cut and carried in her hand ——?"

"A kind of water-lily, is it not?"

"Yes, it is the Sacred Lily. The plant is rooted in the mire at the bottom of the pond, and grows up through the water to the surface. The stem rises in a serpentine curve, and terminates in a flower-bud, which opens with a sigh of delight when the sun strikes upon it, and fills the air with its perfume."

"A sigh, did you say?"

"Yes, a low sweet sound resembling a sigh. The flower is white—'living white'—that is to say, white shot with many colours like the opal. We call it the Sun Lily, or 'Flower of the Soul.'"

"Why 'Flower of the Soul?'"

"Because we say it has the infinite and ever-changing beauty of the soul. It is an emblem of Love, and its manifestations—beauty, genius, holiness. In particular it signifies the birth or awakening of love in the human soul. As the plant may be said to exist for the flower, its chief glory, so the man attains his perfection through love, which confers a boundless and immortal worth upon his life. As the root takes from the soil and the flower brings forth the fruit, so hate feeds upon the ill, and love dies for the good of others. It also represents the human race, for man, and especially woman, may be regarded as the flower of this lower world. Moreover, the entire plant, root, stem, and flower, is symbolical of all creation, and some of our poets have named it the 'Lily of Life.' For as the plant begins in the black earth to end in the sunny ether, so the world, the universe, begins in chaos and darkness, to end in light and order; begins in matter and force, to end in life and spirit—begins in hate and selfishness, to end in love and self-sacrifice—begins in ugliness, to end in beauty. Thus the flower and root stand for the upper and lower limits or poles of nature, and the stalk which joins them for the upward range or path of creation. It is a beautiful stem, curving in opposite ways like a serpent, or the side of a wave; in fact, it is the most beautiful curve we know—it runs like this."

Here Otāré described a flamboyant curve in the air with his finger.

"If I'm not mistaken it is what our artists call the 'line of beauty,'" observed Gazen.

"Oh, indeed!" responded Otāré, with pleased surprise. "Well, with us it is a symbol of the continuous unfolding of things; the graceful progress of development."

"So the path of evolution is the 'line of beauty,'" said the professor.

"Apparently," rejoined Otāré, "and as the ends of the curve point oppositely, we say that a thing has not reached its final stage—that its development is not complete—until it has turned to its opposite. Thus man is not a finished being until hate and selfishness have turned to love and self-sacrifice. The flower of the soul is love, and as the sun is an emblem of the divine love, when the sacred lily opens and displays all its beauty in the sunshine, it means to us that the flower of the soul blooms in the smile of 'The Giver.'"

"I see," said the professor; "and what is done with the flower?"

"It is an offering," replied Otāré, "and after the Priestess of the Lily, or Priestess of the Sun, as we call her, has shown it to the people it will be treasured in the temple, and will never fade."

"Beautiful woman, the priestess! And so young."

"She is barely seventeen. The Priestess of the Sun Lily must be in the flower of her age, and the early dawn of her womanhood. Every year by the popular voice she is chosen from all the maidens of the country for her intelligence, beauty, and goodness. For a year before the ceremony she lives in the temple with her maidens, and never leaves the sacred island, or has any visitors from the outer world. During this period she undergoes a preparation and purification for the fulfilment of her holy office—the culling of the flower. It consists mainly in the study of our sacred writings, the eating of a certain food, and bathing in the waters of a holy fountain, which issues from the rock in a sacred grotto of the island. When the ceremony of cutting the lily is over, and the holy month has expired, that is to say in ten days from now, she will leave the temple and return to her family. Another girl will take her place —the priestess appointed for the coming year—in fact, the maiden who gave her the sickle."

I had listened to this conversation with breathless interest, but without daring to take part in it.

"Will she ever marry?" enquired Gazen.

I waited for the answer with a beating heart.

"Oh, yes," replied Otāré, "why not? She will

marry if she finds a lover whom she can love. There are many who admire Alumion."

"What of yourself?" asked the professor, smiling pointedly. "You seem to know a good deal about her."

"I am her brother."

Nothing more was said, for at this moment the barge was seen coming from behind the temple, after having made a round of the spectators, and presently drew up at the marble stairs. Again the doors swung open, and the maidens reappeared to welcome their mistress with a song of joy. I saw her ascend the steps bearing the lily in her hand, then turn and wave an adieu to the multitude, who responded by a parting hymn as the great purple valves closed together and rapt her from my sight.

CHAPTER X.

ALUMION.

ALUMION—Alumion—I could think of nothing but Alumion. Her very name was music in my ears, and her image in my heart was a perpetual banquet of delight. I had never known such felicity before. My inclination for Miss Carmichael and every other transient affection or interest I may have felt was altogether of a lower strain—with one exception, a boyish admiration for a school girl who died a mere child. The ethereal flame of this new passion seemed to purify all that was earthly, and exalt all that was celestial in my nature. This beautiful land, so green and smiling under a sky of serene azure and snowy wreaths, became as the highest heaven to me, and I wandered about in a dream of ecstacy like one of the blessed gods inebriated with nectar.

I avoided my travelling companions. Their worldly conversation jarred on the mood I was in, and I preferred my own thoughts to their pursuits. As my sole desire was to hear about Alumion, and if possible to see her again, I courted the society of Dinus and Otāré. I knew, of course, that in ten days she would return to her family, but I thought I might be able to visit the temple and perhaps get a glimpse of her. However, I learned from her father that during the sacred festival the temple was closed to the outer world. It was not indeed forbidden to land on the holy island, but it was considered a sacrilege for anyone not having business there to enter the precincts of the temple, excepting on the day of the ceremony which had just taken place. While bound to respect this taboo, I was, nevertheless, drawn by an irresistible attraction to the island, where I frequently spent hours in sailing about the wooded shores, or loitering in the sacred avenue, hoping against hope that I might see her passing by or in the distance. Although I was not so fortunate, I enjoyed the satisfaction of being nearer to her, and as the island seemed a perfect solitude, I could indulge my reverie in peace.

At last I made a discovery. In describing the ceremony of the Flower, Otāré had spoken of a sacred grotto where the priestess went to bathe, and on questioning him further, I ascertained that it was situated on the shore of the island in a bay or inlet to the eastward of the quay, and that she took her customary bath at set of sun.

That afternoon I made a thorough search and found a cavern in the rock close to the beach of a secluded cove which I had overlooked until then. A footpath, winding down the mountain side through the forest led to its mouth, which was overhung and almost hid by a rich creeper with large crimson blossoms. It was evidently the spot mentioned by Otāré, but wishing to make sure, and impelled by curiosity in spite of a more hallowed feeling, I lifted the creeper and was about to peer into the darkness, when a sudden noise within made me jump back with affright. It was the most horrible and excruciating shriek I had ever heard in my life. If anyone by a refinement of cruelty were to compound a torture for the ears, I do not think he could produce anything half so piercing, gruesome, and discordant.

It seemed the cry of an animal—a wild beast—and I began to think I was mistaken in the place; but the sun was near its setting now, and it was too late to seek further afield. I therefore returned to my boat and withdrew under the overarching boughs of some trees where I could see without being seen.

I had not long to wait. Between the flowering shrubs I noticed that a figure—a woman by her undulating grace—was coming down the path. A thin wrap or veil of changing stuff, with gleams of azure and fiery red, was flung about her person. Presently she stepped upon the beach into the mellow gloaming, and stood like a statue, with her eyes bent on the sinking orb, which threw a trail of splendour across the lake.

It was the priestess, and apparently alone. A closer view of her person brought me no disenchantment. Perfect beauty, like the sublime, produces an impression of the infinite, and I only speak the literal truth when I say that she appeared infinitely beautiful to me. Her golden hair, rippling over the delicate ear and gathered into a knot behind, her large violet eyes and blooming white skin, her Grecian profile and stately yet flowing form, might have become an Aphrodite of Xeuxis or Praxiteles; but her serene and gracious countenance beamed with a pure seraphic light which is wanting to the classical goddess, and must be sought in the Madonnas of Raphael. Moreover, she had an indescribable look of girlish innocence, winsome sweetness, and pitiful tenderness, which belonged to none of these ideals, and marked her as a simple, loving, perishable child of earth.

I gazed upon her marvellous beauty with a kind of religious veneration, at once attracted by her womanly charm and awed by her god-like dignity, yet with a strange, a divine state of repose and pure rapture in my heart for which there is no name.

Would that the happiness, the bliss of looking upon her, of being near her, might have lasted for ever!

I knew, however, that she would soon enter the grotto and be lost to me. Should I speak? In this fraternal community what was there to prevent it? Something held me back. Otāré had said that the priestess was isolated from the outer world during her year of office; but that was only a general statement. Mine was a peculiar case. I was a stranger. I did not belong to their world, and was not supposed to know the ins and outs of their customs. Besides, why should custom stand between such a love as mine and its object? Conventional propriety was for the pitiful earth and its wretched abortive passions. Perhaps I should frighten her? No, I did not believe it. In this golden land even the birds seemed fearless. As well think to frighten an angel in Heaven.

While I was debating the question within myself she glanced into the foliage where I was hidden.

How my heart throbbed! I fancied that she saw me, and trembled with emotion; but I was mistaken, for she turned and walked towards the cavern.

Suddenly I remembered the alarming sound within the cave, and breaking through the covert, called after her.

"Take care, take care! There is a wild beast in the grotto. I heard it cry."

She looked round and started when she saw me. The surprise, visible on her face, seemed to melt into recognition.

"It is kind of you to warn me," she responded with a frank smile, "but I am not in danger There is no wild animal inside."

Her low sweet voice was quite in keeping with her beauty. Every note rung clear and melodious as a bell.

"But the awful cry?" I rejoined with a puzzled air.

"Was that of a particular pet of mine," she answered laughingly.

"Pardon me," said I smiling for company, "I am a stranger here, as you can see, and did not know any better."

"You are one of the travellers from another world, are you not?"

"Ah! you have heard of our arrival."

"Oh yes! An event so important was not kept from me. I saw you sitting beside my father on the day of the Flower, and I knew you again. I am afraid our country will seem very odd to you. Have you enjoyed your stay?"

"So much. I cannot tell you how much."

"I hope you will remain with us a long time."

"I should like to stop here for ever."

She blushed and smiled with pleasure at these words, then, raising her arms in a noble salute, inclined her head, and entered the cavern.

I returned to the car in a delirium of happiness. I had seen her again, I had actually spoken with her. *She knew me!* Every detail of her look and accent was indelibly printed on my memory. All next day I wandered about in a kind of transport, feasting on the recollection of what had passed between us, and revolving over my future course of action. In two days the holy time would end, and I should have an opportunity of meeting her at home; but with the chance of seeing her again at the grotto, I could not wait. I was allured towards her by the most delicious fascination. Such a love as mine looked down upon the petty proprieties which keep lovers apart, yet are sometimes so needful in our wicked world. In this noble planet life was free and simple, because it was beautiful and good. I determined to revisit the cove that evening, and if I should see her again, to declare my secret.

Had I counted the cost? With such a passion it is not a question of cost. I was well aware that if she did not reciprocate my affection she would never marry me. Nor did I wish it otherwise. I would not ask her to sacrifice herself for my sake. If, as my heart fondly hoped, she accepted me, I would not allow anything to stand between us for a moment. I would abandon the expedition if necessary, and remain in Venus. If, on the other hand, she refused me as my judgment feared, I would return to the earth as a new man, ennobled by a glorious love, reverencing myself that I was capable of it, cherishing her image in my heart as the ideal of womanhood, and grateful for having seen and known her. Surely a rich reward for all the perils of the journey.

Sunset found me in the cove, not hidden by the leaves as before, but sitting in the boat astrand. She came. To-night her veil was of a golden yellow shading into dark green. A beautiful smile of recognition passed over her face when she saw me, and we greeted one another in the graceful fashion of the country.

I did not speak of the weather or give an excuse for my presence there, as I might have done to a woman of the world. With Alumion I felt that all such artificial forms were idle, and that I could reveal my inmost soul without disguise, in all its naked sincerity.

"I have brought you some flowers," said I, offering her a nosegay which I had picked. "Will you accept them?"

"I thank you," she replied with a beaming smile as she came and took them from my hand. "They are very beautiful, and I shall keep them for your sake."

"For my sake!"

Inspired by love I continued in a voice trembling with emotion,

"Alumion—can you not guess what brings me here?"

A blush rose to her cheek as she bent over the flowers.

"It is because I love you," said I; "because I have loved you ever since I saw you on the day you cut the sacred lily; because I love you—worship you—with all my heart and soul."

She was silent.

"If I am wrong, forgive me," I went on in a pleading tone. "Blame the spell your beauty has cast over me, but do not banish me from your presence, which is life and light to me."

"Wrong!" she murmured, lifting her wondrous eyes to mine. "Can it be wrong to love, or to speak of love? Why should I send you away from me because you love me? Is not love the glory of the heart, as the sun is the glory of the world? Rejoice, then, in your love as I do in mine."

"As you do?"

"Yes, as I do. I should have spoken sooner, but my heart was full of happiness. For I also love you. I have loved you from the beginning."

With a cry of unspeakable joy I sprang from the boat, and would have flung myself at her feet to kiss her hand or the hem of her garment, but she drew back with a look of apprehension.

"Touch me not," she said gravely, "for by the custom of our land I am holy. Until to-morrow at sunset I am consecrated to The Giver."

"Pardon my ignorance," I responded rather crestfallen. "Your will shall be my law. I only wished to manifest my eternal gratitude and devotion to you."

"Kneel not to me," she rejoined, "but rather to The Giver, who has so strangely brought us together. How many ages we might have wandered from world to world without finding each other again!"

"You think we have met before then?" I enquired eagerly, for the same thought had been haunting my own mind. It seemed to me that I had known Alumion always.

"Assuredly," she replied, "for you and I are kindred souls who have been separated in another world, by death or evil; and now that we have met again, let us be faithful and loving to each other."

"Nothing shall separate us any more."

The words had scarcely passed my lips when the same terrible cry which I had heard once before sounded from the interior of the grotto.

Alumion called or rather sang out a response to the cry, which I did not understand, then said to me in her ordinary voice,

"It is Siloo. I must go now and give him food."

I was curious to know who or what was Siloo, but did not dare to ask. She raised her arms gracefully and smiled a sweet farewell.

"Are you going to leave me like that?" said I.

"What would you have?" she answered, turning towards the cave.

"In my country lovers bind themselves by mutual vows."

"What need of vows? Have we not confessed our loves?"

"Will you not tell me when I shall see you again? Will you not say when you will be mine —when you will marry me?"

A blush mounted to her cheek as she answered with a divine glance,

"Meet me at sunset to-morrow, and I will be yours."

As yet I had not mentioned my adventure with Alumion to any of my companions, but that night I said to Gazen, as we smoked our cigars together,

"Wish me joy, old fellow! I am going to be married."

He seemed quite dumbfounded, and I rather think he fancied that I must have come to an understanding with Miss Carmichael.

"Really!" said he with the air of a man plucking up heart after an unexpected blow. "May I ask who is the lady?"

"The Priestess of the Lily."

"The Priestess!" he exclaimed utterly astonished, but at the same time vastly relieved. "The Priestess! Come, now, you are joking."

"Never was more serious in my life."

Then I told him what had happened, how I had met her, and my engagement to marry her.

"If you will take my advice," said he dryly, "you'll do nothing of the kind."

"Why?"

"Have you considered the matter?" he replied significantly.

"Considered the matter! A love like mine does not 'consider the matter' as though it were a problem in Euclid. With such a woman as Alumion a lover does not stop to 'consider the matter,' unless he is a fool."

"A woman—yes; but remember that she is a woman of another planet. She might not make a suitable wife for you."

"I love her. I love her as I can never love a woman of our world. She is a thousand times more beautiful and good than any woman I have ever known. She is an ideal woman—a perfect woman—an angel in human form."

"That may be; but what will her family say?"

"My dear Gazen, don't you know they manage these things better here. Thank goodness, the 'family' does not interefere with love affairs in this happy land! We love each other, we have agreed to be married, and that is quite sufficient. No need to get the 'consent of the parents,' or make a 'settlement,' or give out the banns, or buy a government license as though a wife were contraband goods, or hire a string of four-wheelers, or tip the pew-opener. What has love to do with pew-openers? Why should the finest thing in life become the prey of such vulgar parasites? Why should our heavenliest moments be profaned and spoiled by needless worries—hateful to the name of love? Our wedding will be very simple. We shall not even want you as groomsman or Miss Carmichael as bridesmaid. I daresay we shall get along without cake and speeches, and as for the rice and old boots, upon my word, I don't think we shall miss them."

"And if it is a fair question, when will the—the simple ceremony take place?"

"To-morrow evening."

"To-morrow evening!" exclaimed the professor, taken by surprise. "I thought a priestess could not marry."

"To-morrow at sunset she will be a free woman. Her priesthood will come to an end."

"And—pardon me—but what are you going to do with her when you've got her? Will you bring her home to the car—there is very little room here, as you know. Do you propose to take her to the earth, where I'm afraid she will probably die like a tender plant or a bird of paradise in a cage? Do you think her father would consent to that?"

"We are not going away just yet. There will be time enough to arrange about that."

"Well, we can't stay here much longer. I must get back to my work—and you know we intended to pay a flying visit to Mercury, and if possible to get a closer look at the sun."

"All right. You can go as soon as you like. I shall remain behind. Carmichael will take you to the earth, and then come back here for me."

"You talk as if it were merely a question of a drive."

"I think we have proved that it is not more dangerous to go from one planet to another than it is to get about town."

"If an accident *should* occur. If Carmichael cannot return—"

"I shall be much happier here than I should be on the earth. Even if I had never met Alumion I think I should come back and stay on Venus."

"It is certainly a better world, as far as we have seen, but remember your own words, 'Man was made for the earth.' Don't you think this eternal summer—these Elysian Fields—would pall upon you in course of time? Constant bliss, like everlasting honey, might cloy your earthly palate, and make you sigh for our poor, old, wicked, miserable world, that in spite of all its faults and crimes, is yet so interesting, so variable, so dramatic—so dear."

"Never. With Alumion even Hades would be an Elysium."

"Think of your friends at home, and what you owe to them; how they will miss you."

"I cannot be of much service to them. They will soon forget me."

"Perhaps you are mistaken there," said Gazen, assuming a more serious air. "In any case I for one shall miss you. In fact, to speak plainly, I shall feel aggrieved—hurt. You and I are old friends, and when you asked me to join you in this expedition I was moved by friendship as well as interest. Certainly, I never dreamed that you would desert the ship. I thought it was understood that we should sink or swim together. If you leave us I shan't answer for the consequences. I appreciate the dilemma in which you are placed, but surely friendship has a prior if a weaker claim than love-passion. Surely you owe some allegiance to Carmichael and myself."

"What would you have me do?"

"Only to carry out the original plan of the

voyage. Promise me that you will stick to the ship. Afterwards you can return to Venus and do as you please. Stanley, you know, made his greatest journey into Africa between his engagement and his marriage."

"Very well, I promise."

With an agitated mind I repaired to the tryst next evening and waited for Alumion. How should I break the news to her, and how would she receive it?

The cool airs of the water, and the glorious pageant of the sunset calmed my troubled spirit. All day the serene and beamy azure of the heavens had been plumed with snowy cloudlets of graceful and capricious form, which, as the sun sank to the horizon, were tinged with fleeting glows resembling the iris of a dove's neck, or the hues of a dying dolphin. The great luminary himself was lost in a golden glamour, and a single bright star shone palely through a rosy mist, which covered all the southern sky, like a diamond seen through a bridal veil of gauze.

That lone star was the earth.

Strange to say, I felt a kind of yearning towards it, a yearning as of home-sickness, and it seemed to reproach me for having thought of forsaking it. I wondered what my friends were doing now within that blaze; perhaps they were looking at Venus and speculating on what I was about. How delighted I should be to see them again, and show them my incomparable wife—but could I ever take her there?

Whilst I was musing, the low sweet voice of Alumion thrilled me to the marrow. I turned and saw her. She was dressed to-night in a filmy vesture of opalescent or pearly white, partly diaphanous, and having a deep fringe of gold. There was a pink blush on her cheek and a sparkle of girlish love in her celestial eyes. Never had she seemed more ravishingly beautiful.

> "Beauty too rare for use, for earth too dear."

"You were gazing on the star. You did not hear my coming," she said with a little feminine pout.

"I was thinking of you, darling."

She smiled again.

"Is it not a lovely star?" she said. "We call it the star of Love—the star of the Blest."

"It is my home."

"Your home!" she exclaimed with a look of surprise and wonderment.

"You have heard that I come from another world."

"Yes, but I did not know it was a star. And is that beautiful star your home?"

"Yes, beloved; and I am sorry to say I must return there soon again."

"And I will go! You will take me with you to that fair world!"

I thought of all the crime and folly, the deceit, violence, and wretchedness lurking behind that pure and peaceful ray. Alas! how could I tell her the truth and destroy her illusions. She was innocent as a child, and an instinct warned me to keep the knowledge of evil from her, while a contrary spirit urged me to speak.

"You might not find it so fair as it looks from here."

"I am sure it cannot be an evil world since you come from it. To us it is a sacred star."

"If the inhabitants could see it as I do now, perhaps the sight would make them lead better lives—would shame them into being worthier of their dwelling-place."

"Are they not good?" she asked with a look of wonder and sorrowful compassion. "Then how unhappy they must be."

"Some are good and some are bad. Everything is mixed in our world—the strong and the weak—the rich and the poor—the happy and the miserable."

"But do the good not help the bad?"

"Yes, to a certain extent; but life is a struggle there; every man for himself; and the good very often find it hard to secure a little happiness for themselves."

"How can they be happy when they know that others are suffering and in want, that others are bad? I long to go and help them."

"Darling, you are an angel, and I adore you; but, believe me, you alone could do very little. One has already come and taught us how to love and cherish each other, that the strong should help the weak, the rich give to the poor, and the happy comfort the wretched. His followers believe that He came from Heaven, and yet after nineteen hundred years I am afraid that some of them do not fully understand the plain meaning of His words, or else find it convenient to ignore them."

"But many of us will go there. We will bring the sinful and the suffering over here to Womla and make them happy."

"I am touched by your simple faith in us, dearest. It does you honour, but I fear it is mistaken. What would you say if the very people you had saved and befriended were to turn round and take your country from you, perhaps even destroy you? Such ingratitude is not unknown in our world."

"If they are so wicked they have the more need of help."

"In any case, darling, I cannot take you with me, for the vessel we came in is too small; but I will come back as soon as possible and stay with you in Womla. How happy we shall be!"

"In Womla—no. We should not be quite at rest."

"Then we shall seek out some desert star where we can live only for each other."

"You do not understand me. Neither in Womla nor in a desert star could we be happy in a selfish love, knowing that others were in pain."

"Better I had not spoken of my world at all."

"No, a thousand times no!" cried Alumion with fervour. "For you have opened up to me a new source of happiness—of blessedness which I have never known before. Only let us go together to your world and minister to the unfortunate."

"Well, darling, we will think of it; but see! the sun has set and you are free again. I came to marry you, but since I must return so soon to my own world, perhaps it would be well to postpone the ceremony until I come back here."

"Why should we do that?"

Evidently she had no idea of the dangers of the journey, or how long it would take.

"If anything should happen to me. If I should die and never return."

"Ah! do not speak of that. The Giver will preserve you."

"But life is uncertain."

"Beloved, I shall never love another but you; therefore, let us unite ourselves, as we are already united in heart and soul, henceforth and forever. Come!"

With these words she turned and glided towards the sacred grotto. I held aside the flowering creeper which hung over the entrance like a curtain, and followed her within. To my great surprise the interior was neither dark nor dusky, but filled with a soft and luscious light from myriads of glow-worms and fire-flies of various colours, which glimmered on the walls like tiny electric lamps, or sparkled in the facets of the gems and spars depending from the roof. Judging by their shape and tint I imagine that some of these incrustations are native crystals of the diamond and ruby, the sapphire, topaz, and emerald. In a deep recess or alcove on one side a spring of clear water gushed from the rock into a natural basin of sinter, enamelled inside and out with the precious opal. Owing perhaps to the minerals through which it had passed the liquid shed a delicious perfume in the air, and made a bath fit for the goddess of beauty.

I had scarcely time to look about me when a strange and wonderful melody of most entrancing sweetness echoed through the cavern.

"Siloo, Siloo!" cried Alumion softly, and the music, which I cannot compare to any earthly strain, ceased in a moment. Presently I was more than startled to see in the gloomier background of the cavern a great white serpent glide like a ghost along the floor and come straight towards us. His milk-white body was speckled all over with jewelled scales, and shone with a pale blue phosphorescence; his eyes blazed in his head like twin carbuncles, and in spite of my instinctive dread of snakes, I could not help admiring his repulsive beauty. Presently he reared his long neck, and faced us with his forked tongue playing out and in. I shrank back, for I thought he was about to spring upon me; but Alumion, laughing gaily at my fears, stepped quickly up to him, and stroked him with her hand. The serpent laid his head caressingly upon her shoulder and emitted a low faint note of pleasure.

Alumion then took a shallow dish or patera, and, filling it from a vase which she carried with her set it upon the floor for the snake to feed.

"You don't seem to be afraid of that gruesome reptile," said I pleasantly.

"Oh, no," she replied smiling. "Siloo knows me very well."

"Tell me, was it he who made the music a little while ago?"

"Yes, and also the noise which alarmed you the first night you wandered here. The music comes from his head, and the noise is from his tail. That is why we call him Siloo."

The word, as nearly as I can translate it, means harmony, order, measure, proportion, in the Womla tongue.

"Does he always live in this cave?"

"Yes, he is a sacred animal with us, and long ago was worshipped and consulted by our forefathers, and those who preceded them in the island."

"Is he very old?"

"None can tell how old. Some say he is immortal. Others think he is only the offspring of the snake worshipped by our forefathers. He is guardian of the sacred fountain whose waters we are about to drink."

When she had spoken, Alumion tripped to the flowing spring, and, taking a cup which was standing on the edge of the basin, filled it from the pellucid stream.

"Give me your hand," she murmured, holding out her own, and lifting her celestial eyes, so full of love and tenderness, to mine. It was a dainty hand, plump, lilywhite, and dimpled, with tapering fingers; and as I felt her warm and silk-soft touch for the first time, my soul melted within me, and my whole being thrilled with delight. Her rosy lips parted with pleasure, and a delicate blush mantled her blooming cheeks and full white throat.

I gazed in rapture on her divine countenance, so like a speaking flower, the image of a beautiful soul on which neither sorrow, care, nor passion had ever left a trace.

She raised the cup, and having sipped of the water, handed it to me in silence. I sought the place where her lips had touched the brim and drank. Now whether it was phantasy or some foreign ingredient I cannot tell, but the water seemed to taste like nectar, and to run through all my veins like wine.

The glamour of the lights and the perfume of the waters wrought upon my senses, and, yielding to the intoxication of my love, I caught Alumion to my arms.

Suddenly the most appalling noise rent the air, and caused me to spring back from my bride in terror. It came from the rattlesnake. His grisly body swayed to and fro, his gaping mouth displayed all its horrid fangs, and his large eyes burned like two red-hot coals.

"Siloo, Siloo!" cried Alumion hastily in a tone of command. "Down, Siloo!"

The serpent at once obeyed her voice and retired again to his dish.

"He thought I was going to harm you," I exclaimed, not without a sense of relief. "Or perhaps he was jealous of me."

"Remember this is holy ground," responded Alumion.

"Forgive me," I said, feeling her reproof. "My love—your beauty—must be my excuse."

"We must part now," she continued, with a blinding glance and a ravishing smile. "I have some last offices to perform here. We shall meet to-morrow at my father's house."

On my way home the blood coursed through my veins like an immortal ichor of the gods, full of sweet and inextinguishable fire. Inebriated with the cup of bliss which I had only tasted, I began to repent me of my promise to leave Womla.

"To-morrow Alumion will be mine," I reflected, "but for how long? A few days at the most. It is too bad!"

An idea struck me.

"Gazen," said I that night as soon as I had a convenient opportunity to speak with him, "I have married Alumion."

"Married her!" he exclaimed, completely taken aback.

"Yes, that is to say, I have gone through the formal ceremony of marriage. I have drunk of the cup."

"But you promised me you would do nothing of the kind."

"I said I would go back to the earth with you, and I will keep my word. But I must say that since I agreed to your wishes in the matter, I think you owe me some concession, and I want you to leave me in Womla while you go on to Mercury, and then come back here to pick me up. That will give me a longer honeymoon."

"Impossible, my dear fellow—quite impossible," replied the professor. "Venus will be too far out of our way home. We have no oxygen to waste, and can't go hunting you in your love affairs all round the solar system."

"Very well, then, I shall stay behind."

"But, my dear fellow—"

"Say no more about it. I have made up my mind."

CHAPTER XI.

THE FLYING APE.

It was broad day when I awoke, and oppressively warm in the little cabin. My first thoughts were of Alumion, the consecration of our loves, and my resolution to abide in Venus. In getting up I felt so light and buoyant that for a moment I fancied I must be giddy, but on reflection I ascribed the sensation to the intoxication of passion, and the exhilarating atmosphere of the planet. I looked out of a window towards the blessed island of my dreams, and to my blank amazement found that *it was gone!* I could neither see anything of the lake, the square, nor the town, but only a bare and rugged platform of weathered rocks, and the cloudy sky above it.

What was the matter? Had Gazen and Carmichael taken it into their heads to make an excursion, such as we had often planned, in order to observe something more of the country? Yes, that was it, no doubt.

Under the circumstances I was far from pleased with them for having carried me off without asking my leave, knowing as they should have done, that I would be eager to rejoin Alumion; but experience of travel had taught me that a man must not expect to have it all his own way, and should know when to let his companions have theirs, and above all things to keep his temper. I, therefore, decided to take their behaviour in good part, more especially as we could always return to the capital as quickly as we had come from it.

Apparently there was nobody in the car but myself. Wondering, and perhaps a trifle uneasy at the dead stillness, I dressed rapidly and went outside.

The welkin was wholly overcast with dense, murky vapours, which totally hid the sun, and the air was excessively hot, moist, and sultry as before a thunderstorm—an unusual phenomenon in Womla. Black boulders and crags, speckled with lichens, and carpeted with coarse herbage, shut out the prospect on every side but one, where the edge of the platform on which the car was resting ran along the sky. I saw it all now. Gazen and Carmichael had made a journey to the extreme verge of the country; to the very summit of the precipice which surrounded the Crater Land.

Picking my steps over the rough rocks like one who treads on air, I hastened to the brink of the platform. If the car were on the further side of the summit I should be able to see the wide ocean, but if, as I fondly hoped, it were on the hither side, I should enjoy a far-off glimpse of the city and its holy island, which had become a heaven to me. How different was the scene which met my view!

I was looking away over a vast plain towards a distant range of volcanic mountains. A broad river wound through the midst between isolated volcanoes, curling with smoke, and thick forests of a sable hue, or expanded into marshy lakes half lost in brakes of grisly reeds, on the margin of which living monsters were plashing in the mud, or soaring into the air on dusky pinions.

My first shock of surprise passed into a fearful admiration for the savage and gloomy grandeur of the primeval landscape; but as that feeling wore away the old irritation against my fellow-travellers came back. From all I had heard or seen there was no such place as this in Womla, and as it dawned upon me that they had migrated to some other island, or perhaps continent in Venus, I forgot my good resolution, and shouted indignantly,

"Gazen, Gazen! Hallo there! Hallo!"

There was no response, and the dead silence that swallowed up my voice was awful. Had anything happened to my companions, and was I left alone in this appalling solitude? Was I in my right senses, or was I not? I shouted again at the very pitch of my voice, and this time an answering cry came to my relief. On turning in the direction from which it proceeded, I observed Professor Gazen coming slowly towards me, round a mass of turretted rocks.

"What is the meaning of all this?" I demanded petulantly, as he came near, gingerly stepping from stone to stone.

He made no reply, but seemed to be meditating what he would say.

"A nice trick you've played me! Wherever have we got to?"

"Mercury," replied Gazen coolly.

"*Mercury!*" I exclaimed, fairly astounded. "Impossible!"

"Not at all."

"Oh, come!" said I sarcastically, "that won't do. A joke is a joke; but I'm not in a merry mood this morning."

"So I see. A laugh would do you good."

"Well, where are we?"

"In Mercury."

"What nonsense!" I ejaculated. "Last night I went to bed in Venus, and you want me to believe that I've woke up on Mercury. Tell that to the marines."

"Last night you say; but do you know how long you have slept? And have you forgotten that we are now so near the sun—that the attraction of the sun on the car has assisted the machines to propel us through the intermediate space?"

I had not thought of that.

"Then it is true."

"Of course."

"And why have you come here—what authority—what right—had you to carry me off in this manner without my consent?" I burst out angrily. "You knew I had made up my mind to stay in Venus. I took you into my confidence and told you about my love affair. Why have you betrayed that confidence, and kidnapped me like a slave or a lunatic?"

"Hear me, old friend," said Gazen softly. "We have all noticed a decided change in you of late—ever since the day of the ceremony on the island. You have been like a different person—absent in your mind—incoherent in your speech—abrupt in your manner. You have forsaken your old friends completely, and apparently lost all interest in their doings, all desire for their company. In short, you have behaved like a man beside himself, distraught. We could not make it out, and we had many anxious consultations about the matter. I wondered whether you had had a sunstroke. Carmichael suggested that the stimulating air of Venus had affected your brain. Miss Carmichael alone suspected that you were in love; but I would not believe her. I had been so much in your society without having seen anything to justify her suspicion, and you yourself had never breathed a word to lend it colour. Carmichael and I sought to question you about your health, and the influence of the sun and air upon you, while Miss Carmichael tried to draw you on the subject of the ladies. All in vain. We could not solve the mystery, and as your condition was evidently growing worse and worse, we resolved to leave the planet. Although it was not in the original programme, we had sometimes talked of extending our journey to Mercury, so as to visit all the inferior planets, and give me an opportunity of getting as near the sun as possible for my observations, and this project was made the pretext for hastening our departure.

"We submitted the plan to you, and you know the rest. After you had given us your word of honour that you would break with the lady and return home with us for the sake of your friends, after we had made all our preparations to start, you came back at the eleventh hour, and declared that you had made up your mind to stay behind. If anything had been wanted to prove to us that you were hopelessly infatuated—hypnotised—mad—it would have been that; and as we were morally bound to fetch you back with us, we took the bull by the horns, and carried you off in spite of yourself."

"You had no business to do anything of the kind," I replied hotly. "I am chiefly responsible for this expedition."

"True; but you forget that Carmichael is the nominal leader, by your own agreement, and we are all to some extent under his orders. I, too, was bound in honour to bring you safe home if I could."

"Bound in honour to take care of *me!* You treat me like a baby."

"People don't come away on such an adventure as ours without a tacit if not a formal understanding to protect each other to the best of their ability, and besides, I had given my word to your friends that I would do my best to help you through. When you come to your senses you will acknowledge that we did right."

Despite my excusable anger and vexation, the calm and friendly explanation of the professor was not without its effect on me. It was true that I had broken my promise to my fellow-travellers; true that Carmichael was commander of the expedition. I was myself at fault. And yet what a disappointment! What would Alumion think of me! After all my vows of eternal fidelity, uttered as they had been in that sacred spot, I had sneaked away like a thief in the night.

"I shall go back to Venus," said I, in a determined manner.

"Tut, tut," said Gazen, with a good-natured smile; "you had better give up that idea. You are clearly the victim of hypnotic influence—of suggestion. By-and-by it will lose its hold on you, and you will regain your freedom of action."

"Never!" I exclaimed, with all the energy of my soul. "My dear Gazen, you are quite mistaken in supposing anything of the kind. I was never saner in my life. Nay, it is only now that I know what it is to be sane; what life was meant to be.

Hypnotic suggestion! Pshaw! I know what I am doing as well as you do. I am not a fool. I am only seeking my own happiness—and hers—I tell you that a single moment in her society is worth a whole lifetime on the earth. What do I say? A lifetime? An eternity. Heaven itself were nothing to me without her. I would not take it as a gift. I shall go back. I must go back. I cannot live without her."

"Take time to consider at all events," said Gazen, somewhat impressed by my vehemence. "In the meantime let us join Miss Carmichael. She is beyond the rocks there sketching the valley."

We walked in that direction.

"You may return to the earth," said I; "but on the way you must drop me at Venus."

Gazen had no opportunity of answering, for just at that moment we were startled by a piercing shriek from behind the crags, and rushing, or rather bounding forward, saw a sight that made our very blood run cold.

A flying monster, with enormous bat-like wings and hanging legs, was evidently swooping down on Miss Carmichael, as she stood beside her easel on the brow of the cliff.

"Run for your life!" roared Gazen, dashing towards her with frantic speed.

Alas! she did not hear him, or else she was fascinated by the approaching horror, and rooted to the spot. He was still several hundred yards from her, but owing to the feebleness of gravity on the planet he was so preternaturally light and nimble that he might have covered the distance in a minute or so, had he been more accustomed to control his limbs, and the ground been smoother. As it was he leaped high into the air, and rebounded from the stones like an india-rubber ball, at the risk of spraining his ankles or breaking his neck, while brandishing his arms, and firing his pistol, and hooting with all his force of lung to frighten away the monster.

Too late. The huge leathery wings of the dragon overshadowed the shrinking form of the girl, and the talons of its drooping feet caught in her dress. She made one desperate, but futile effort to free herself from its terrible clutch, and, screaming loudly for help, was borne away over the abyss of the valley as easily as a lamb is carried by an eagle.

"Oh, Heaven!" cried Gazen, stopping with a gesture of despair.

He was deeply moved, and pale as death; but he did not altogether lose his head.

What was to be done?

"The car—the car!" he exclaimed. "We must follow her in the car. Keep your eye on the beast while I go for it."

Carmichael was fast asleep in his cabin, after his long weary vigil during the passage from Venus, but the car was quickly put in motion, and I jumped on board just as it cleared the brink of the precipice.

The dragon, which had the start of us by a mile or more, was apparently steering for the mountains on the other side of the valley. Notwithstanding its enormous bulk, and the dead weight hanging from its claws, it flew with surprising speed, owing to the weakness of gravity and the vast spread of its wings.

I shall never forget that singular chase, which is probably unparalleled in the history of the universe. A prey to anxiety and the most distressing emotions, we did not properly observe the marvellous, the Titanic, I had almost said the diabolical aspect of the country beneath us, and still we could not altogether blind ourselves to it. Colossal jungles, resembling brakes of moss and canes five hundred or a thousand feet in height—creeks as black as porter, gliding under their dank and rotting aisles—mountainous quadrupeds or lizards crashing and tearing through their branches —one of them at least six hundred feet in length, with a ridgy back and long spiky tail, dragging on the ground, a baleful green eye, and a crooked mouth full of horrid fangs, which made it look the very incarnation of cruelty and brute strength—black lakes and grisly reeds as high as bamboo—prodigious black serpents troubling the water, and rearing their long spiry necks above the surface—gigantic alligators and crocodiles resting motionless in the shallows, with their snouts high in the air—hideous toads or such-like forbidding reptiles, many with tusks like the walrus, and some with glorious eyes, crouching on the banks or waddling in the reeds, and so enormous as to give variety to the landscape—volcanic craters, with red-hot lava simmering in their depths, and emitting fumes of sulphur, which might have choked us had we not closed the scuttles—while over all great dragons and other bat-like animals were flitting through the dusky atmosphere like demons in a nightmare.

Little by little we gained upon our quarry, but being afraid to run him too close for fear that he might drop his victim, we kept at a safe distance behind him, yet within rifle range, and near enough to make a prompt attack when he should settle on the ground.

At length we reached the other side of the valley, and found to our intense satisfaction that the monster was making for a rocky ledge on the shoulder of an extinct volcano, where we could see the yawning mouth of what appeared an immense cavern.

"That is probably his den," said Gazen, who was now as collected as I have ever seen him. Nevertheless all his faculties were on the stretch. His keen grey eye was everywhere, and his active mind was calculating every chance. I felt then as I had often felt before that in action as well as in thought the professor was a man of no common mark.

The event showed that his surmise was correct, for soon after he had spoken the dragon uttered a startling cry—a kind of squawk like that of a drake, but much louder, hoarser, shriller—and alighted on the ground.

"There is not a moment to lose," said Gazen. "We must attack him before he enters the cave."

Certainly the darkness inside the cavern would give the beast a great advantage, and although we might succeed in killing him, we could scarcely hope to find Miss Carmichael alive. Was she alive now? I had my doubts, but I kept them to myself. Since she had been carried away she had not given the smallest sign of life, not even when the dragon settled. Perhaps, however, she had merely lost her senses through fright, and was still in a dead faint.

We might have fought the creature from the air, but we had decided to assail him on the solid ground, because we should thus be able to scatter and take him in the flank, if not in the rear.

While Carmichael landed his car the astronomer and I kept a sharp watch on the beast, all ready to fire at the first movement which seemed to threaten the safety of the young girl, who was lying motionless at the bottom of a slope or talus which led up to the mouth of the cavern. Freed from his burden the dragon now stood erect, and a more awful monster it would be difficult to conceive. He must have been at least forty feet in stature, yet he gave us an impression of squat and sturdy strength.

I have called him a dragon, but he was not at all like the dragons of our imagination. With his great bullet head and prick ears, his beetling brows and deep sunken eyes, his ferocious mouth and protruding tusks, his short thick neck and massive shoulders, his large, gawky, and misshapen trunk, coated with dingy brown fur, shading into dirty yellow on the stomach, his stout, bandy legs armed with curving talons, and his huge leathern wings hanging in loose folds about him, he looked more like an imp of Satan than a dragon.

Hitherto he had not appeared to notice his pursuers; but now that he was freer to observe, the grating of the car upon the rocks caught his attention. He turned quickly, and stared at the apparition of the vessel, which must have been a strange object to him; but he did not seem to take alarm. It was the gaze of a jaguar or a tiger who sees something curious in the jungle —vigilant and deadly if you like, but neither scared nor fierce.

We lost no time in sallying forth, all three of us, armed with magazine rifle, cutlass, and revolver. Mr. Carmichael in the middle, I on the lower, and Gazen on the upper side, or that nearest to Miss Carmichael. The rocks around were slippery with ordure, and the sickening stench of rotting skeletons made our very gorge rise. Suddenly a loud squeaking in the direction of the cave arrested us, and before we had recovered from our surprise, nearly a dozen young dragons, each about the size of a man, tumbled hastily down the slope, and rushed upon the lifeless form of Miss Carmichael.

"Great Scott, there's the whole family," muttered

Gazen between his teeth, at the same time bringing his rifle to the shoulder, and firing in quick succession.

The foremost of the crew, which had already flung itself upon the prey, was seen to spring head over heels into the air, and fall back dead ; another lay writhing in agony upon the ground, and uttering strangely human shrieks ; whilst the others, terrified by the noise, turned and fled back helter-skelter to the cave.

The old one, roused to anger by the injury done to his offspring, snarled ferociously at his enemies and, drawing himself to his full height, made a furious dash for Gazen.

Our rifles cracked again and again ; the monster started as he felt the shots, and halted, glaring from one to another of us like a man irresolute. Purple streams were gushing from his head and sides ; he attempted to fly, and ran towards the brink of the ledge ; but ere he could gain sufficient impetus to launch himself into the air, he staggered and fell heavily to the ground, with his broken wings beneath him.

Gazen, quicker than her father, flew towards Miss Carmichael, and bent over her.

"Is she alive?" enquired Carmichael, in breathless and trembling accents.

"Yes, thank God," responded Gazen fervently; as he raised her hand to his lips and kissed it.

There were tears of joy in his eyes, and I knew then what I had long suspected, that he loved her.

Suddenly a loud croak in the distance caused us to look up, and we beheld another dragon on the wing, coming rapidly towards us from a pass among the mountains. There was not a moment to be lost, and Gazen, taking Miss Carmichael in his arms, we all hurried on board the car, eager to escape from this revolting spot.

CHAPTER XII

SUNWARD HO!

"BY the way," said Gazen to me, "I've got a new theory for the rising and sinking of the sun behind the cliffs at Womla—a theory that will simply explode Professor Possil, and shake the Royal Astronomical Society to its foundations."

The astronomer and I were together in the observatory, where he was adjusting his telescope to look at the sun. After our misadventure with the flying ape, we had returned to our former station on the summit of the mountain, to pick up the drawing materials of Miss Carmichael; but as Gazen was anxious to get as near the sun as possible, and being disgusted with the infernal scenery as well as the fœtid, malarial atmosphere of Mercury, we left as soon as we had replenished our cistern from the pools in the rock.

"Another theory?" I responded. "Thought you had settled that question."

"Alas, my friend, theories, like political treatises, are made to be broken."

"Well, what do you think of it now?"

"You remember how we came to the conclusion that Schiaparelli was right, and that the planet Venus, by rotating about her own axis in the same time as she takes to revolve around the sun, always keeps the same face turned to the sun, one hemisphere being in perpetual light and summer, whilst the other is in perpetual darkness and winter?"

"Yes."

"You remember, too, how we explained the growing altitude of the sun in the heavens which culminated on the great day of the Festival, by supposing that the axis of the planet swayed to and from the sun so as to tilt each pole towards the sun, and the other from it, alternately, thus producing what by courtesy we may call the seasons in Womla?"

"Yes."

"Well, judging from the observations I have made, we were probably right so far; but if you recollect, I accounted for the mysterious daily rise and set of the sun, if I may use the words, by changes in the density of the atmosphere bending the solar rays, and making the disk appear to rise and sink periodically, though in reality it does nothing of the kind. A similar effect is well-known on the earth. It produces the 'after glow' on the peaks of the Alps when the sun is far below the horizon; it sometimes makes the sun bob up and down again after sunset, and it has been known to make the sun show in the Arctic regions three weeks before the proper time. I had some difficulty in understanding how the effect could take place so regularly."

"I think you ascribed it to the interaction of the solar heat and the evaporation from the surface."

"Quite so. I assumed that when the sun is low the vapours above the edge of the crater and elsewhere cool and condense, thus bending the rays and seeming to lift the sun higher; but after a time the rays heat and rarefy the vapours, thus lowering the sun again. It seemed a plausible hypothesis and satisfied me for a time, but still not altogether, and now I believe I have made a discovery."

"And it is?"

"That Venus is a wobbler."

"A wobbler?"

"That she wobbles—that she doesn't keep steady—swings from side to side. You have seen a top, how stiff and erect it is when it is spinning fast, and how it wobbles when it is spinning slow, just before it falls. Well, I think something of the kind is going on with Venus. The earth may be compared to a top that is whirling fast, and Venus to one that has slowed down. She is less able than the earth to resist the disturbing attraction of the sun on the inequalities of her figure, and therefore she wobbles. In addition to the slow swinging of her axis which produces her 'seasons,' she has a quicker nodding, which gives rise to day and night in some favoured spots like Womla."

"After all," said I, "'tis a feminine trait. *Souvent femme varie.*"

"Oh, she is constant to her lord the sun," rejoined Gazen. "She never turns her back upon him, but if I have not discovered a mare's nest, which is very likely, she becks and bows to him a good deal, and thus maintains her 'infinite variety.'"

The cloudy surface of Mercury now lay far beneath us, and the glowing disc of the sun, which appeared four or five times larger than it does on the earth, had taken a bluish tinge—a proof that we had reached a very great altitude.

"What a magnificent 'sun-spot!'" exclaimed the professor in a tone of admiration. "Just take a peep at it."

I placed my eye to the telescope, and saw the glowing surface of the disc resolved into a marvellous web of shining patches on a dimmer background, and in the midst a large blotch which reminded me of a quarry hole as delineated on the plan of a surveyor.

"Have you been able to throw any fresh light on these mysterious 'spots?'" I enquired.

"I am more than ever persuaded they are breaks in the photosphere caused by eruptions of heated matter, chiefly gaseous from the interior—eruptions such as might give rise to craters like that of Womla, or those of the moon, were the sun cooler. No doubt that eminent authority, Professor Sylvanus Pettifer Possil, regards them as aerial hurricanes; but the more I see, the more I am constrained to regard Sylvanus Pettifer Possil as a silly vain asteroid."

While Gazen was yet speaking we both became sensible of an unwonted stillness in the car.

The machinery had ceased to vibrate.

Our feelings at this discovery were akin to those of passengers in an ocean steamer when the screw stops—a welcome relief to the monotony of the voyage, a vague apprehension of danger, and curiosity to learn what had happened.

"Is there anything wrong, Carmichael?" asked Gazen through the speaking tube.

There was no response.

"I say, Carmichael, is anything the matter?" he reiterated in a louder tone.

Still no answer.

We were now thoroughly alarmed, and though it was against the rules, we descended into the machinery room. The cause of Carmichael's silence was only too apparent. We saw him lying on the floor beside his strange machine, with his head leaning against the wall. There was a placid expression on his face, and he appeared to slumber; but we soon found that he was either in a faint or dead. Without loss of time we tried the first simple restoratives at hand, but they proved of no avail.

Gazen went and called Miss Carmichael.

She had been resting in her cabin after her trying experience with the dragon, and although most anxious about her father, and far from well herself, she behaved with calm self-possession.

"I think the heat has overcome him," she said, after a quick examination; and truly the cabin was insufferably hot, thanks to the machinery and the fervid rays of the sun.

We could not open the scuttles and admit fresh air, for there was little or none to admit.

"I shall try oxygen," she said on reflecting a moment.

Accordingly, while Gazen, in obedience to her directions began to work Carmichael's arms up and down, after the method of artificial respiration which had brought me round at the outset of our journey, she and I administered oxygen gas from one of our steel bottles to his lungs by means of a makeshift funnel applied to his mouth. In some fifteen or twenty minutes he began to show signs of returning animation, and soon afterwards, to our great relief, he opened his eyes.

At first he looked about him in a bewildered way, and then he seemed to recollect his whereabouts. After an ineffectual attempt to speak, and move his limbs, he fixed his eyes with a meaning expression on the engines.

We had forgotten their stoppage. Miss Carmichael sprang to investigate the cause.

"They are jammed," she said after a short inspection. "The essential part is jammed with the heat. Whatever is to be done?"

We stared at each other blankly as the terrible import of her words came home to us. Unless we could start the machines again, we must inevitably fall back on Mercury. Perhaps we were falling now!

We endeavoured to think of a ready and practicable means of cooling the engines, but without success. The water and oil on board was luke-warm; none of us knew how to make a freezing mixture even if we had the materials; our stock of liquid air had long been spent.

Miss Carmichael tried to make her father understand the difficulty in hopes that he would suggest a remedy, but all her efforts were in vain. Carmichael lay with his eyes closed in a kind of lethargy or paralysis.

"Perhaps, when we are falling through the planet's atmosphere," said I, "if we open the scuttles and let the cold air blow through the room, it will cool the engines."

"I'm afraid there will not be time," replied Gazen, shaking his head; "we shall fall much faster than we rose. The friction of the air against the car will generate heat. We shall drop down like a meteoric stone and be smashed to atoms."

"We have parachutes," said Miss Carmichael, "do you think we shall be able to save our lives?"

"I doubt it," answered Gazen sadly. "They would be torn and whirled away."

"So far as I can see there is only one hope for us," said I. "If we should happen to fall into a deep sea or lake, the car would rise to the surface again."

"Yes, that is true," responded Gazen; "the car

is hollow and light. It would float. The water would also cool the machines and we might escape."

The bare possibility cheered us with a ray of hope.

"If we only had time, my father might recover, and I believe he would save us yet," said Miss Carmichael.

"I wonder how much time we have," muttered Gazen.

"We can't tell," said I. "It depends on the height we had reached and the speed we were going at when the engines stopped. We shall rise like a ball thrown into the air and then fall back to the ground."

"I wonder if we are still rising," ejaculated Gazen. "Let us take a look at the planet."

"Don't be long," pleaded Miss Carmichael, as we turned to go. "Meanwhile, I shall try and bring my father round."

On getting to the observatory, we consulted the atmospheric pressure gauge and found it out of use, a sign that we had attained an altitude beyond the atmosphere of Mercury, and were now in empty space.

We turned to the planet, whose enormous disc, muffled in cloud, was shining lividly in the weird sky. At one part of the limb a range -of lofty mountain peaks rose above the clouds and chequered them with shadow.

Fixing our eyes upon this landmark we watched it with bated breath. Was it coming nearer, or was it receding from us? That was the momentous question.

My feelings might be compared to those of a prisoner at the bar watching the face of the jury-man who is about to deliver the verdict.

After a time—I know not how long—but it seemed an age—the professor exclaimed,

"I believe we are still rising."

It was my own impression, for the peak I was regarding had grown as I thought smaller, but I did not feel sure, and preferred to trust the more experienced eyes of the astronomer.

"I shall try the telescope," he went on; "we are a long way from the planet."

"How far do you think?"

"Many thousand miles at least."

"So much the better. We shall get more time."

"Humph! prolonging the agony, that's all. I begin to wish it was all over."

Gazen directed his instrument on the planet, and we resumed our observations.

"We are no longer rising," said Gazen af er a

time. "I suppose we are near the turning-point."

As a prisoner scans the countenance of the judge who is about to pronounce the sentence of life or death, I scanned the cloudy surface underneath us, to see if I could discover any signs of an ocean that would break our fall, but the vapours were too thick and compact.

Every instant I expected to hear the fatal intelligence that our descent had begun.

"Strange!" muttered Gazen by-and-by, as if speaking to himself.

"What is strange?"

"We are neither rising nor falling now. We don't seem to move."

"Impossible!"

"Nevertheless, it's a fact," he exclaimed at the end of some minutes. "The focus of the telescope is constant. We are evidently standing still"

His words sounded like a reprieve to a condemned man on the morning of his execution, and in the revulsion of my feeling I shouted,

"Hurrah!"

"What can it mean?" cried Gazen.

"Simply this," said I joyfully. "We have reached the 'dead-point,' where the attraction of Mercury on the car is balanced by the attraction of the sun. It can't be anything else."

"Wait a minute," said Gazen, making a rapid calculation. Yes, yes, probably you are right. I did not think we had come so far; but I had forgotten that gravitation on Mercury is only half as strong as it is on the Earth or Venus. Let us go and tell Miss Carmichael."

We hurried downstairs to the engine room and found her kneeling beside her father, who was no better.

She did not seem much enlivened by the good news.

"What will that do for us?" she enquired doubtfully.

"We can remain here as long as we like, suspended between the Sun and Mercury," replied Gazen.

"Is it better to linger and die in a living tomb than be dashed to pieces and have done with it?"

"But we shall gain time for your father to recover."

"I am afraid my father will never recover in this place. The heat is killing him. Unless we can get further away from the sun he will die, I'm sure he will."

Her eyes filled with tears.

"Don't distress yourself, dear Miss Carmichael,

please don't," said Gazen tenderly. "Now that we have time to think, perhaps we shall hit upon some plan."

An idea flashed into my head.

"Look here," said I to Gazen, "you remember our conversation in your observatory one day on the propelling power of rockets—how a rocket might be used to drive a car through space?"

"Yes; but we have no rockets."

"No, but we have rifles, and rifle bullets fired from the car, though not so powerful, will have a similar effect."

"Well?"

"The car is now at rest in space. A slight impulse will direct it one way or another. Why should we not send it off in such a way that in falling towards Mercury it will not strike the planet, but circle round it; or if it should fall towards the surface, will do so at a great slant, and allow the atmosphere to cool the engines."

"Let me see," said Gazen, drawing a diagram in his note-book, and studying it attentively. "Yes, there is something in that. It's a forlorn hope at best, but perhaps it's our only hope. If we could only get into the shadow of the planet we might be saved."

As delay might prove fatal to Carmichael, and

since it was uncertain whether he could right the engines in their present situation, we decided to act on the suggestion without loss of time. Gazen and I calculated the positions of the rifles and the number of shots to be fired in order to give the required impetus to the car. The engine-room, being well provided with scuttles, was chosen as the scene of our operations. A brace of magazine rifles were fixed through two of the scuttles in such a way that the recoil of the shots would urge the car in an oblique direction backwards, so as to clear or almost clear the planet, allowance being made for the forward motion of the latter in its orbit. Needless to say, the barrel of each rifle was packed round so as to keep the air in the car from escaping into space.

At a given signal the rifles were discharged simultaneously by Gazen and myself. There was little noise, but the car trembled with the shock, and the prostrate man opened his eyes.

Had it produced the desired effect? We could not tell without an appeal to the telescope.

"I'll be back in a moment," cried Gazen, springing upstairs to the observatory.

"Do you feel any better, father?" enquired Miss Carmichael, laying her cool hand on the invalid's fevered brow.

He winked, and tried to nod in the affirmative.

"Were you asleep, father? Did the shock rouse you?"

He winked again.

"Do you know what we are doing?"

Before he could answer the foot of Gazen sounded on the stair. He had left us with an eager, almost a confident eye. He came back looking grave in the extreme.

"We are not falling towards Mercury," he said gloomily. "*We are rushing to the sun!*"

I cannot depict our emotion at this awful announcement which changed our hopes into despair. Probably it affected each of us in a different manner. I cannot recollect my own feelings well enough to analyse them, and suppose I must have been astounded for a time. A vision of the car, plunging through an atmosphere of flame, into the fiery entrails of the sun, flashed across my excited brain, and then I seemed to lose the power of thought.

"Out of the frying-pan into the fire," said I at last, in frivolous reaction.

"His will be done!" murmured Miss Carmichael, instinctively drawing closer to her father, who seemed to realise our jeopardy.

"We must look the matter in the face," said Gazen, with a sigh.

"What a death!" I exclaimed, "to sit and watch the vast glowing furnace that is to swallow us up come nearer and nearer, second after second, minute after minute, hour after hour."

"The nearer we approach the sun the faster we shall go," said Gazen. "For one thing, we shall be dead long before we reach him. The heat will stifle us. It will be all over in a few hours."

What a death! To see, to feel ourselves roasting as in an oven. It was too horrible.

"Are you certain there is no mistake?" I asked at length.

"Quite," replied Gazen. "Come and see for yourself."

We had all but gained the door when Miss Carmichael followed us.

"Professor," she said, with a tremor in her voice, and a look of supplication in her eyes, "you will come back soon—you will not leave us long."

"No, my darling—I beg your pardon," answered Gazen, obeying the impulse of his heart. "God knows I would give my life to save you if I could."

In another instant he had locked her in his arms.

I left them together, and ascended to the observatory, where Gazen soon afterwards rejoined me.

"I'm the happiest man alive," said he, with a beaming countenance. "Congratulate me. I'm betrothed to Miss Carmichael."

I took his proffered hand, scarcely knowing whether to laugh or cry.

"It seems to me that I have found my life in losing it," he continued with a grim smile. "Saturn! what a courtship is ours—what an engagement—what a bridal bed! But there, old fellow, I'm afraid I'm happier than you—alone in spirit, and separated from her you love. Perhaps I was wrong to carry you away from Venus—it has not turned out well—but I acted for the best. Forgive me!"

I wrung his hand in silence.

"Now let us take a look through the telescope," he went on, wiping his eyes, and adjusting the instrument. "You will see how soon it gets out of focus. We are flying from Mercury, my friend, faster and faster."

It was true.

"But I don't understand how that should be," said I. "The firing ought to have had a contrary effect."

"The rifles are not to blame," answered Gazen. "If we had used them earlier we might have saved ourselves. But all the time that we were discussing ways and means, and making our preparations to shoot, we were gradually drifting towards the sun without knowing it. We overlooked the fact that the orbit of Mercury is very far from circular, and that he is now moving further away from the sun every instant. As a consequence his attractive power over the car is growing weaker every moment. The car had reached the 'dead-point' where the attractive powers of the sun and planet over it just balanced each other; but as that of the planet grew feebler the balance turned, and the car was drawn with ever accelerating velocity towards the sun."

"Like enough."

"I can satisfy you of it by pointing the telescope at a sun-spot," said Gazen, bringing the instrument to bear upon the sun. "You will then see how fast we are running to perdition. I say—what would our friends in London think if they could see us now? Wouldn't old Possil snigger! Well, I shall get the better of him at last. I shall solve the great mystery of the 'sun-spots' and the 'willow leaves.' Only he will never know it. That's a bitter drop in the cup!"

So saying, he applied his eye to the telescope, his ruling passion strong in death. For myself, as often as I had admired the glorious luminary, I could not think of it now without a shudder, and fell a prey to my own melancholy ruminations.

So this was the end! After all our care and forethought, after all our struggles, after all our success, to perish miserably like moths in a candle, to plunge headlong into that immense conflagration as a vessel dives into the ocean, and is never heard of more! Not a vestige of us, not even a charred bone to tell the tale. Alumion—our friends at home—when they admired the sun would they ever fancy that it was our grave—ever dream that our ashes were whirling in its flames. The cry of Othello, in his despair, which I had learned at school, came back to my mind—

> "Blow me about in winds! Roast me in sulphur!
> Wash me in steep-down gulfs of liquid fire!"

Regrets, remorse, and bitter reflections overwhelmed me. Why had we not stayed in Venus? Why had we come to Mercury? Why had we endeavoured to do so much? What folly had drawn me into this mad venture at all? No, I could not say that. I could not call it folly which had brought me to Alumion. I had no regret, but on the contrary an unspeakable joy and gratitude on that score. But why had we attempted to approach so near the sun, daring the heat, which had jammed our engines, and disabled our best intellect; risking the powerful attraction that was hurrying us to our doom?

Suddenly a peculiar thrill shook the car. With a bounding heart I started to my feet and dashed into the engine-room. It was true then. Yes, it was true. *The engines were at work, and we were saved!*

CHAPTER XIII.

HOME AGAIN.

WE owed our salvation to Mr. Carmichael. The firing of our magazine rifles, followed by the news of our perilous situation, had roused him from his lethargy. Although still unable to speak, he had contrived by means of his eyes to make his daughter understand that he wished another dose of oxygen. When she was about to administer it, he called her attention to the fact that in expanding as it issued from the cylinder, the gas became very cold. She caught his meaning instantly, and on applying the gas to the sensitive parts of the machinery had succeeded in cooling and releasing them.

It seems that Carmichael, in order to save time, had been working the engines at an unusually high speed, which, together with the heat of the sun, had caused them to jam. Their enforced rest had of itself allowed them to cool somewhat, and by reducing the speed until we reached a cooler region, they did not stick again.

Carmichael recovered from his illness, and the journey to the earth was accomplished without accident. We landed safely on some undiscovered islands in the Arctic Circle, and after a flying visit to the North Pole in the vicinity, we bore away for England, keeping as high over the sea as possible to escape notice. Going southward we passed through all sorts of weather, thick snow, hurricanes of wind and rain, dry or wet fogs, and so forth ; but it made no difference to us. Crossing Spitzbergen, the car was frosted over with ice needles, which, however, were soon thawed by a warmer current of air. Between Iceland and the coast of Norway we glided through a magnificent aurora borealis that covered the whole sky with a luminous curtain, and made us fancy we had floated unawares into the fabulous Niffleheim of the old Scandinavian gods. Near the Faroe Islands we dashed into a violent thunderstorm, and were almost deafened by the terrific explosions, or blinded by the flashes of lightning. Otherwise we could enjoy both of these electrical displays without fear, as the metallic shell of the car was a good protective screen. Certainly our flying machine would be an excellent means of making observations in meteorology, from the sampling of cirrus cloud to the chasing of a tornado.

The first sign of man we saw was a ship rolling in a storm off the Hebrides; but apparently she was not in distress, else we should have gone to her succour. How easy with such a car to rescue lives and property from sinking ships, and even patrol the seas in search of them!

The sun was setting in purple and gold as we approached the English coast, and although at our elevation we were still in sunshine, the twilight had begun to gather over the distant land. The first sound we heard was the moaning of the tide along the shore, and the mournful sighing of the wind among the trees. Hills, fields, and woods lay beneath us like a garden in miniature. The lamps and fires of lonely villages and farmhouses twinkled like glow-worms in the dusk. A railway train, with its white puff of smoke and lighted carriages, seemed to be crawling like a fiery caterpillar along the ground; but in a few moments we had left it far behind. As it grew darker and darker we descended nearer to the surface. A herd of sheep stood huddled on the grass, and stared at us; a flock of geese ran cackling into a farmyard; the watch-dog barked and tugged furiously at his chain ; a little boy screamed with fright.

"That sounds homely," said the professor to Miss Carmichael and myself, who were standing with him on the gallery outside the car. "It's the sweetest music I've heard for many a day. Certainly Venus was a charming place, but I for one am jolly glad to get home again."

Yes, I must confess that I too felt a deep and tranquil pleasure in returning to the familiar scenes and the beloved soil of my infancy.

"You don't seem to care much for Venus," said Miss Carmichael to Gazen. "Probably if you had been born there you would have liked it better."

"That may be. If you would like a place, it is well to be born in it."

"Perhaps if you are a good boy you will go to Venus when you die."

"I'm afraid it won't suit my mental constitution. They don't care for science there, and I don't care for anything else. Mars would fit me better, I imagine."

"Venus is my favourite," said Miss Carmichael.

"Well, then, it's good enough for me," responded Gazen.

Their talk set me thinking of Alumion, and my

strange fancy that I had known her in another world. Suddenly it occurred to me that in many of her ways and looks she bore a singular resemblance to my first love, who had died in childhood. That was nearly seventeen years ago. Seventeen —it was just the age of Alumion. Could it be possible that she and Alumion were one and the same soul?

"I should like to go back to Venus," said Miss Carmichael. "We can go there now at any time."

"Of course we can," replied Gazen; "and to Mars as well. Your father's invention opens up a bewildering prospect of complications in the universe. So long as each planet was isolated, and left to manage its own affairs, the politics of the solar system were comparatively simple; but what will they be when one globe interferes with another? Think of a German fleet of ether-ships on the prowl for a cosmical empire, bombarding Womla, and turning it into a Prussian fortress, or an emporium for cheap goods."

"Father was talking of that very matter the other night," said Miss Carmichael, "and he declared that rather than see any harm come to Womla he would keep his invention a secret—at all events for a thousand years longer."

We had glided rapidly across the Black Country, with its furnaces and forges blazing in the darkness, and now the dull red glow of the metropolis was visible on the horizon. Half-an-hour later we descended in the garden of Carmichael's cottage, and found everything as snug as when we had left it.

* * * * *

Leaving my fellow-travellers there, I took the train for London, and was driven to my club, where I intended to sleep. It was a raw wet evening, and in spite of a certain joy at being home again, I could not help feeling that my heart was no longer here, but in another planet. After the sublime deserts of space, and the delightful paradise of Womla, the busy streets, the blinding glare of the lamps, the splashing vehicles, the blatant newspaper men, the swarms of people crossing each other's paths, and occasionally kicking each other's heels, everyone intent on his own affairs of business or pleasure, were disenchanting, to say the least. I seemed to have awakened from a beautiful dream, and fallen into a dismal nightmare.

In the smoking-room of the club the first person I saw was my friend the Viscount, who was sitting just where I had left him on the night we started for Venus, with his glass of toddy before him, and a cigar between his lips.

"Hallo!" he exclaimed on seeing me. "Haven't seen you for some time—must be nearly two months. Been abroad? You look brown."

"Yes."

"Well, suppose we finish our game of chess."

"With pleasure."

"You remember the wager—a thousand to a hundred sovereigns that I win."

He was the better player, and although I had a slight advantage in the game as it stood, I was by no means certain of winning, especially as I was tired and sleepy; but ever since my sojourn in Venus, my intellect had been unusually clear and active. I played as I had never played before, and in three moves had won the wager.

"That will pay my travelling expenses," said I, pocketing his cheque.

* * * * *

I ought perhaps to mention that Professor Gazen carried out his intention of reading a paper to the Royal Astronomical Society on his alleged discovery of a diurnal nutation or "wobbling" of the planet Venus; but I regret to say that owing to preconceived opinions and personal prejudices, his ingenious theory met with a reception far below its merits. By the terms of our agreement he was forbidden to divulge the secret of our expedition until my own account appeared, but some telescopic observations he had made since coming home had provided him with independent proofs.

"Do you think Professor Possil will be present?" said I to him, as we dined together before we went to the meeting.

"Sure to be," replied Gazen. "He never misses an opportunity of attacking me. 'Tis the nature of the animal. But I flatter myself I shall get the laugh on him this time."

The hall was full. The hearty welcome of the Fellows showed their high appreciation of Professor Gazen, and made me feel quite proud of his acquaintance. They listened to his discourse on the movements of Venus, and his new hypothesis, with all the solemnity of a Roman senate deliberating on the destiny of a nation. When he had finished in a salvo of applause, the president, a man of grave and dignified demeanour, as became his office, complimented the author on his communication, which from the startling novelty of the subject would, he believed, give rise to an interesting discussion, and after calling on Professor Possil, he resumed his chair. That illustrious man, whose insignificant appearance belied his fame, responded to the invitation with a show of reluctance, from a conspicuous place in the front row of the audience, and immediately assailed the new hypothesis in his most uncompromising fashion.

"Never in his experience of the Society," he said, "and never perhaps in the history of astronomy, had an alleged discovery of such magnitude and consequence been promulgated on the strength of such flimsy evidence;" and after traversing in detail all the arguments of his opponent, he declared it his firm conviction that the effects which Professor Gazen had thought fit to advance as a "discovery," were neither more nor less than an optical illusion, not to say a mental hallucination.

Judging from the applause which greeted his remarks, the majority of his hearers were evidently of the same opinion.

A grim smile settled on my companion's face, and I could see that he maintained his temper with increasing difficulty, as one speaker after another delivered his mind in much the same sarcastic style of criticism.

At length his turn came to make a reply.

"Mr. President and gentlemen," said he with an air of smiling confidence, "at this late hour I do not propose to occupy the meeting with a refutation of all the various comments of the distinguished Fellows who have spoken; but as my learned friend, Professor Possil, has thought fit to charge me with bringing my discovery before the Society on insufficient grounds, I think it right to say that I possess much more conclusive evidence, which for the present, circumstances have prevented me from laying before you."

"Mr. President," exclaimed the celebrated Possil, starting to his feet, "I should like to ask whether it is altogether in good faith for a Fellow of this Society to bring forward what he calls a discovery, and keep back the most important part of the proof. Might I enquire of the author of the paper what is the nature of this suppressed evidence?"

"Simply that I have been there," answered Gazen, forgetting his promise to me in the excitement of the combat.

"Where?" demanded the astonished Possil.

"Venus."

There was a loud burst of sceptical laughter.

"I think, sir," said Professor Possil to the Chair, with exasperating coolness, "I think, sir, that after the astounding revelation of the learned professor, we shall be perfectly justified in concluding on sufficient evidence that the professor's head, and not the planet Venus, has been 'wobbling' of late."

"What I say is true," cried Gazen, nettled at this rude insinuation.

Cries of "Order, order," "withdraw," "apologise," resounded on every side.

'I cannot apologise for the truth," retorted Gazen hotly.

"Mr. President," continued the pugnacious and imperturbable Possil, "I venture to submit that the preposterous assertions we have just heard are better adapted to a meeting of the Fellows of Colney Hatch than of this Society, and I beg to move that our unfortunate friend be called upon to leave the meeting in charge of some responsible person, who will conduct him safely to his home, and deliver him into the custody of his friends."

"Come on! They're a pack of fools!" cried Gazen to me hoarsely, as, followed by the jeers of his companions, he arose and left the room.

* * * * *

I have only to add that Professor Gazen and Miss Carmichael are about to be married. For myself, as soon as the ceremony is over I shall return to Venus and Alumion.

THE END.

I have only to add that Professor Gazen and Miss Carmichael are about to be married. For myself, as soon as the ceremony is over I shall return to Venus and Alumion.

THE END.

the astounding revelation of the learned professor, we shall be perfectly justified in concluding on sufficient evidence that the professor's head, and not the planet Venus, has been 'wobbling' of late."

"What I say is true," cried Gazen, nettled at this rude insinuation.

Cries of "Order, order," "withdraw," "apologise," resounded on every side.

'I cannot apologise for the truth," retorted Gazen hotly.

"Mr. President," continued the pugnacious and imperturbable Possil, "I venture to submit that the preposterous assertions we have just heard are better adapted to a meeting of the Fellows of Colney Hatch than of this Society, and I beg to move that our unfortunate friend be called upon to leave the meeting in charge of some responsible person, who will conduct him safely to his home, and deliver him into the custody of his friends."

"Come on! They're a pack of fools!" cried Gazen to me hoarsely, as, followed by the jeers of his companions, he arose and left the room.

* * * * *